Advance Praise for *West of the Moon*

"A masterfully spun tale of perilous joy for any true story lover's greedy little heart. Savor." —Rita Williams-Garcia, Newbery Honor-winning author of *One Crazy Summer*

"I love this book! *West of the Moon* is compelling, enchanting, and honest, an astounding blend of fiction and folklore that celebrates the important things in life—loyalty, devotion, courage, and the magic of stories. I think you will love it, too." —Karen Cushman, Newbery Medal-winning author of *The Midwife's Apprentice*

"A gorgeous reminder that we all live and die by the stories we tell—and by the stories we choose to be in." —William Alexander, National Book Award-winning author of *Goblin Secrets*

"Margi Preus has produced a magical novel about a feisty young girl . . . Writing with great imagination and wit, she also shows how Astri creatively uses . . . Norwegian folk and fairy tales to ground herself and give herself hope." —Jack Zipes, editor of *The Golden Age of Folk and Fairy Tales: From the Brothers Grimm to Andrew Lang*

To Henry
Reach for the Moon!

MARGI PREUS

Amulet Books
NEW YORK

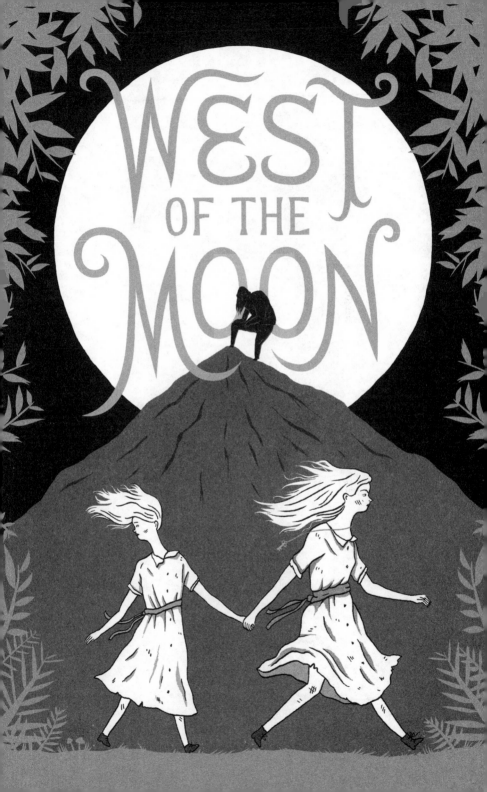

Library of Congress Cataloging-in-Publication Data

Preus, Margi.
West of the moon / Margi Preus.
pages cm
Summary: In nineteenth-century Norway, fourteen-year-old Astri, whose cruel aunt sold her to a mean goatherder, dreams of joining her father in America.
Includes bibliographical references.
ISBN 978-1-4197-0896-1 (alk. paper)
[1. Human trafficking—Fiction. 2. Emigration and immigration—Fiction. 3. Norway—History—19th century—Fiction.] I. Title.
PZ7.P92434We 2014
[Fic]—dc23
2013023250

Text copyright © 2014 Margi Preus
Interior illustrations © 2014 Lilli Carré
Book design by Sara Corbett

Image on page 198 courtesy of Vesterheim Norwegian-American Museum, Decorah, Iowa. Images on pages 206 and 207 courtesy of Luther College Archives, Decorah, Iowa.

Printed and bound in U.S.A.
10 9 8 7 6 5 4 3 2 1

Amulet Books are available at special discounts when purchased in quantity for premiums and promotions as well as fundraising or educational use. Special editions can also be created to specification. For details, contact specialsales@abramsbooks.com or the address below.

THE ART OF BOOKS SINCE 1949

115 West 18th Street
New York, NY 10011
www.abramsbooks.com

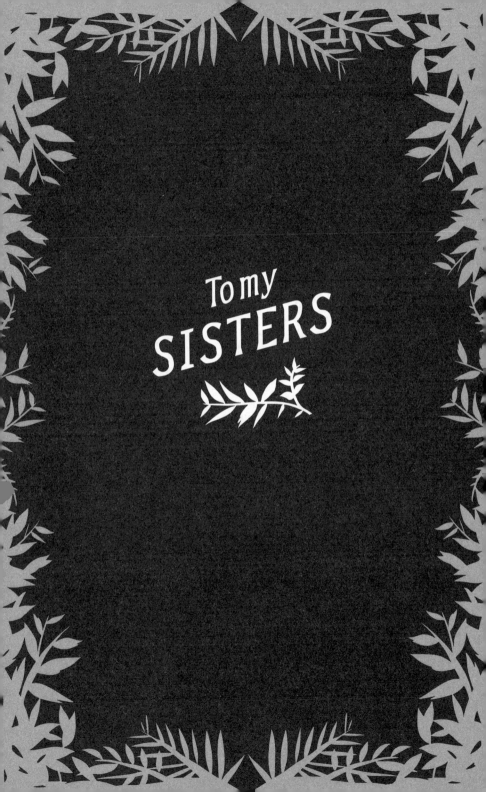

To my
SISTERS

CONTENTS

I

The Goat Farm

II

Flight

◆ III ◆

The *Columbus*

The Goat Farm

MID-NINETEENTH-CENTURY NORWAY

White Bear King Valemon

The fire hisses, then snaps, and the dog looks up from his place on the hearth. His hackles rise; a low growl escapes him. Aunt looks up from her knitting. A hush falls on the room—that curious feeling of something-about-to-happen seizes us. As for my cousins, the eldest holds her needle in midair; the middle one falls quiet, taking her hands away from the loom and setting them in her lap. The twins are silent, for once.

And me? Somewhere deep within me, my heart pounds, distant as an echo, as if it is already far away, in another place and another time.

There's a story I know about a white bear who came and took the youngest daughter away with him, promising the family everything they wanted and more, if the father would only let him take her. In the story, the family was sitting in their house when something passed by outside the window. Hands to their hearts, they all gasped. Pressed up against the window was the face of a bear—a white bear—his wet nose smearing the glass, his eyes searching the room. As he moved past, it was as if a splotch of sunlight momentarily penetrated the gloom.

3

That is *that* story. In *my* story I am sitting in the house with my aunt and uncle and cousins when something passes by outside the window. In the twilight it is just a dark shape. The room dims as the shadow goes by, and even after it passes, the darkness lingers, as if the sun has gone for good.

Aunt sets her knitting in her lap. She tries not to smile, holding her lips firm, but the smile makes its way to her forehead, and her eyebrows twitch with satisfaction.

My stomach works its way into a knot; my breath catches halfway down my throat.

A sharp knock on the door makes us all jump. Aunt gets up, smooths her skirt, and crosses to open it. My cousins glance at me, then away when I return their look. Greta isn't here. She must be hiding, which is just as well.

The man has to stoop to come in the low doorway, then, when inside, unfolds himself, but something makes him seem still stooped. It's a hump on his back. Even standing up straight it's there, like a rump roast oddly perched on one shoulder. I can't stop staring at it. He's chesty like an old goat, and wiry everywhere else. He's got the billy goat's scraggly beard and mean little eyes like black buttons. As ill-mannered as a goat, too, for he doesn't bother to take off his hat.

He squints around the room with his glittery eyes without saying *"God dag"* or *"Takk for sist."* No, his jaw works away at his cud of tobacco, and when he finally opens his mouth

4

to reveal his stained teeth, it's to bleat out, "Which is the girl, then?"

His beady eyes gleam as they drift over pretty Helga's curves, glint as they take in Katinka's blonde braids, almost sparkle when they behold Flicka's ruddy cheeks. But when Aunt points to me, he turns his squint on me and his eyes turn flat and dark. "Well, I hope she can work," he grunts.

"Aye," says Aunt. "She's as hearty as a horse."

"Her name?"

"Astri."

"How old?"

"Thirteen. Fourteen by summer."

"Not a handful, I hope," he says. "I don't care for trouble in a girl. Don't care for it!" This he proclaims with a shake of his shaggy head and a stamp of his walking stick.

"She'll be no trouble to you, Mr. Svaalberd," Aunt lies. "Get your things, Astri."

My limbs are so numb I can barely climb the ladder into the loft. There is Greta, sitting on the lump of my straw mattress, her face wet with tears.

"Little sister," I say softly, and we embrace. I'd been able to keep from crying till now, when I hear her trembling intake of breath. "Greta," I whisper, "stop crying. Don't make me cry. I can't show Mr. Goat any weakness. You show a billy goat you're afraid of him, and he'll be lording it over you day and night."

Greta stops sniffling and takes my hands. "Big sister," she says, "you must be stronger—and meaner—than he is!"

"Aye, that's so," I say. "I shall be." I dry her tears with my apron and swipe at my own, too.

Her tiny hands press something into mine, something heavy, wrapped with a child's clumsiness in a piece of cloth. "You take this, Astri," she says.

I unwrap it to see our mother's silver brooch. "Keep it," Greta whispers. "Aunt will take it away if she finds out about it, you know."

I nod. Greta is already so wise for such a tiny thing. Too wise, maybe.

"Little sister," I tell her, holding my voice steady, "Papa will send for us, and then we'll go to America to join him."

Greta drops her head and nods. She doesn't want me to see she's crying, but her shoulders are shaking.

"Astri!" Aunt yells up the stairs. "Don't dawdle!"

I kiss the top of Greta's head and place my hand on her face for just a moment—all I dare, or risk a broken heart.

Down the ladder I go to stand by the door, my bundle under my arm. I can't help but notice there are now two shiny coins glinting on the table, along with a large, lumpy package. My cousins are eyeing the coins with the same intensity that the dog is sniffing the package. Now I know how much I'm worth: not as much as Jesus, who I'm told was sold for thirty pieces of silver. I am worth two silver coins and a haunch of goat.

Uncle comes and tucks a wisp of hair behind my ear, almost tenderly. "I'm sorry, Astri," he says. "It can't be helped."

That's all there is for a good-bye, and then out the door I go.

⁑⁂⁑

I n the story, the young maid climbed upon the white bear's back, and he said, "Are you afraid?"

No, she wasn't.

"Have you ever sat softer or seen clearer?" the white bear asked.

"No, never!" said she.

Well. That is a story and this is my real life, and instead of White Bear King Valemon, I've got Old Mr. Goat Svaalberd. And instead of "Sit on my back," he says "Carry my bag," and on we troop through the darkening woods, the goatman in front and me behind, under the weight of his rucksack and my own small bundle of belongings. The only thing white is the snow—falling from the sky in flakes as big as mittens. Strange for it to be snowing already, while leaves are still on the trees. It heaps up on them, making the branches droop, and piles up on the goatman's hump until it looks like a small snowy mountain growing out of his back.

"Aren't you afraid of the trolls who come out at night?" he says.

"I'm not afraid," I tell him, though it's a lie. It's twilight; the sun has slipped behind the mountains, and the shadows begin to dissolve into darkness. The time of day when honest, churchgoing people go home to bed.

He breaks off a rowan twig and gives it to me. "Tuck that into your dress," says he, "for protection."

I stumble along behind the goatman, trying to memorize every boulder and tree, every bend in the trail so I can find my way back. But evening is ending and the full night is coming on. We leave a dotted line of footprints behind us, which are rapidly filled in with snow. By morning there won't be a trace of us left behind.

⁂

When the youngest daughter arrived at the bear's house, it was a castle she found, with many rooms all lit up, rooms gleaming with gold and silver, a table already laid, everything as grand as grand could be. Anything she wanted, she just rang a little silver bell, and there it was.

Not so for me, for when I come to the lair of Mr. Goat, it is a hovel, and filthy inside. The walls are soot-covered, and the fire-place so full of cinders that every time the door opens or shuts, ashes and smoke puff out into the room, enough to make you choke. A hard lump—ash, I suppose—settles in my throat.

The goatman's dog—Rolf, his name is—plunks himself down on the hearth and trains his yellow eyes on me.

Old Goatbeard lights a smoky fire in the fireplace and dumps a cold, greasy hunk of mutton on the table. Then he saws off the heel of a loaf of bread with a big, wide-bladed knife—the only thing shiny in the whole place, polished clean by the bread it slices.

When I scowl at the bread, he says, "Oh, a princess, are we? I suppose you're accustomed to pork roast and applesauce every night."

I say no, for of course we never had any such thing and most of the time no mutton, either, but at least our table was clean and what bread we had wasn't gray with ash and covered with sooty fingerprints.

With the last bit of bread, I swallow the lump that's been stuck in my throat. It slides down and lodges in my chest, where it stays, a smooth, cold stone pressed next to my heart.

Now it is time to sleep, and the goatman shows me my little bed in the corner.

Never trust a billy goat, Astri!

I know it, and so when Svaalberd goes outside to the privy, I sneak quietly to the table and take the heavy knife with the gleaming blade. Lacking the silken pillows with gold fringe that the girl got at King Valemon's castle, I tuck my own little bundle under my head. And under the bundle I slide the knife.

Work

In the morning, I am awakened by a sharp kick to my backside.

"What a worthless lass you are!" the goatman growls. "Look! The day is half dead, and you lie abed like a princess. I'm not feeding you for nothing. Up now and to your tasks."

And so my day begins: milking, hauling, washing, scrubbing, chasing goats, feeding goats, catching goats, avoiding ornery goats. These are the saddest bunch of neglected animals you've ever seen. It nearly makes me weep—their coats matted and tangled, their ribs jutting out, since all they've been eating is sticks. Seems that nobody bothered to cut them hay. So, along with all the other chores, I can see I'll be gathering fodder all winter, too.

So the weeks pass. I've mucked out the goats' shed and trimmed their hooves and pulled the burrs out of their coats. The leaves have dropped from the trees, and the early snow has melted, turning the farmyard into a muddy mess, most of which gets tracked into the house and has to be swept out again by me.

From time to time I get—I don't know how to describe it—a strange feeling that makes me prickle all over. "I feel as if someone is watching me," I tell the goatman.

"Someone is," he says. "It's me. I've got my eye on you, make no mistake!"

So the days go by.

"Daydreaming again, Astri?" Goatbeard interrupts my thoughts, scowling at me.

What am I thinking? Papa can't come all the way back from America. For all I know, once you're there, you can't ever return.

"Where do Aunt and Uncle live?" I ask, without looking up from my milking.

"You know yourself. You were there," says Svaalberd. He's examining the gate of the does' pen to try to figure how Snowflake keeps getting out. That nanny goat is always standing somewhere you don't expect. She'll have her face in the window, or you'll see her wandering around off on a hill somewhere. So far, the goatman hasn't puzzled it out, and I'm not about to tell him how she does it. Right now, he is putting so much concentration into his search that he is talking to me instead of telling me to hold my tongue or shut my trap or just applying the back of his hand to some portion of my head like he usually would.

"Yes, but where do they live from here?" I continue.

"A far piece. You know yourself, you walked it."

"Yes, but what direction is it from here?"

He stops and looks at me, his eyes little slits. "Why do you want to know?"

"Maybe I would like to go home for a visit," I say.

"Maybe you would doesn't mean that maybe you will," he says. "The work here doesn't stop because you want to go sip tea with the Queen."

"I never said a single thing about sipping tea with the Queen. I just want to go home and see my sister. And I don't see anything wrong with it."

"I'll tell you what's wrong with it," he says, launching himself toward me and taking my braid in his filthy fist. "What's wrong with it is that I hired you to work for me and not trot home as if it were Christmas any day of the week." He yanks on my braid so that my head tips back and I have to look at his face upside down, which, it turns out, is just as ugly as it is right-side up.

"If you hired me, then when do I get my pay?" I reply to his forehead.

"You're lucky to get your bed and board, and I've heard just about enough out of you." He drops the braid and ends the conversation with a slap to the back of my head. If I keep prodding him, I'll end up with a black eye, so I bite my lip—hard. Sometimes I have to bite my lip so hard it bleeds.

Every day is like this: Work work work, bite my tongue

or get slapped, and finally it is night again. Maybe, I think, if I were to run away, night would be the time to do it. But night-time is different than the daytime; it's almost like a different place, or maybe a different world altogether, a world said to be inhabited by *huldrefolk*—the hidden people.

Nonetheless, every night I go outside and wonder: Can these nighttime beings be any worse than the devil I live with now? And will this night be the night I am brave enough?

Like tonight. On my way out the door, I lift the latch slowly. I don't glance at the goatman for fear he is watching me. The dog cocks an ear but doesn't open his eyes.

When I pry open the door, of course it lets out a squawk.

"Where you going, girl?" the goatman growls.

"To use the privy," I answer. "Where do you think?"

"That's enough mouth from you," he says.

I let the door bang shut behind me, and I crunch across the frosty ground—not all the way to the outhouse—and stop. The moon overhead has a big white ring around it, like a puddle of cream within a puddle of milk.

I stare out at the dark wall of trees that circle the farm, opening my eyes as wide as I can, trying to peer past the dark-ness. I could walk away right now, and just walk downhill. Even-tually I would come to *something*. A farm, a village, a river . . .

If I'm going to go, I should go now. Once it snows for good, I'll be stuck here for the winter.

But, oh! It is so dark. And quiet in a way it never is in the daytime. Tonight is the quietest yet, so hushed that there is nothing to be heard at all. Nothing but a soft *whirr*, like the thrumming of my own heart, yet somehow far away.

I hold my breath, listening. Where *is* it coming from?

"Girl, what are you doing out here?" It's the goatman, standing in the doorway.

"I hear something strange," I call back to him.

"You hear me telling you to get back inside, is what you hear, or your backside will smart!" he says with a snort.

In I go and climb into my bed. I unwrap Mama's brooch from its cloth wrapping and trace my fingers over it. It's covered in depressed discs like tiny silver spoons. You'd think it would make me remember Mama, but nothing comes of it. I don't even remember her face. Mostly, I remember Papa and the stories he told of Soria Moria and the castle that lies east of the sun and west of the moon. In the story the girl dreamed of a golden wreath that was so lovely she couldn't live unless she got it.

If I could have any wish, I wouldn't squander it on a golden wreath. I might wish for a pair of shoes not so worn out or stockings not so full of holes. What I really want most— well, it's impossible, so there's no use wishing it, or even thinking of it, though sometimes I can't help it. To have my family all together again, whole and complete, that's what I dream of, and I guess that's sort of like a golden wreath. At least, it's as impossible a thing to get as that.

Usually I'm so tired at night, I collapse and dream of nothing. And it's a good thing, too, because nothing is exactly what I get from old Goatbeard.

"You'd best be careful out there at night," he says from the gloom of his corner.

"Why?" I ask.

"Why!" he snorts. "You know yourself the forest is full of *huldrefolk*, the invisibles. 'Tis said they are the children Eve was so ashamed of that she hid them from God. And God said, 'Let those who were hidden from me be hidden from all mankind,' and so they and all their children stay so, even to this day."

"And so they are invisible," I add, "and we can't see them, and they can't see us."

"There are times when the veil parts, and it's possible to see into the other side," the goatman says. "There's no wall that separates us from them, 'tis just the barest veil." He lowers his voice to a dark whisper. "And there are times those folk live side by side with us, whether we know it or not." He grunts and rolls over. "Don't think it can't happen!" he says, and after a few moments, begins to snore.

I touch the log wall by my bed. Are there really hidden people out there? Are they real? Or just made up to keep girls like me from running away?

The Drop of Tallow

In the morning, the first thing out of Svaalberd's mouth is "Have you stolen the knife again, *mus*?" He calls me that—mouse—when he's being friendly. Otherwise it's "dog" or "cow" or "rat" or "pig." I doubt if I am human anymore, by the names he calls me.

I hand Svaalberd the knife, and he slices off some dried mutton, thin slices you can see through, and he carves off a curling slice of brown cheese. He hands me two slices of bread, one for the cheese and one for the meat. This is my breakfast.

It's better than I got at Aunt and Uncle's.

There was no mutton there, and sometimes we had cheese, but often we didn't. And the bread was sometimes made of bark.

There, I've said it. That's how poor we were. We had to eat bark bread. Still, I'd rather be back at Aunt and Uncle's starving with Greta.

Every Sunday morning, old Goatbeard drags his oak chest over to the table, where he fumbles for his keys, puts a key in the lock, and with a *click*, unlocks the chest. He digs down

16

inside it, and I hear the rustle of paper and an enticing *clinkity jingle.*

"There's some fine things in that chest, I shouldn't wonder," I say one morning.

"There's more than you think," he says. "Inside this box, girl, lies prodigious power."

I mouth the word he says: *prodigious.*

"It means a powerful much, is what. In this box lies the power to conjure up and put down the devil and get him to do all that you command. Herein lies the power to cure diseases, remove curses, find buried treasure, and turn back the attacks of snakes and dogs. You stay away from this chest, if you know what's best for you," he says. Then he pulls out his Bible.

"Is it the Holy Book I'm to stay away from?" I ask him.

"Nay," he says, "'tis something else. But nothing for the likes of you."

He then commences to read aloud from his Bible. I say "read," but look at him! How his eyes are pretending to move along the paper, and how he now and then turns a page when it occurs to him. I watch the ropy vein in his neck pulse when he starts in to read brimstone and hellfire—the same vein that pops out when he's about to give me a thrashing. He puts on a good show, but I know he can't read.

"Where did you learn those stories?" I ask him.

"I learnt them from here!" he exclaims. "I'm reading them straight out of the book!"

"Hmmf," I sniff, and study the space between the cheese and the bread, wishing there was some butter to fill that in.

He drones on about Esau and Jacob and how Esau was the hairy one and Jacob was the smooth one and how one day Jacob killed a couple of goats and put their skins over himself and went into his old, blind father's tent bent on trickery of some sort. Meantime, I drift off and start thinking about what sort of trickery I might use on old Goatbeard himself and how to weasel my way out of here.

There are some troubles. It was so dark and snowy when we came from Aunt and Uncle's, I don't even know which direction to go. If Greta and I were really to run away, we would need food for any sort of journey, maybe money, too, and how would I get either one?

There's food in the storehouse, I know, for Svaalberd goes out there with rounds of crisp flatbread I've made and returns with hanks of goat. I suppose there's grain and cheeses and meats, smoked or not, and I don't know what else, as I'm never allowed inside. He keeps the place locked tight, and the key hangs on his heavy iron ring, all a-clatter with keys.

But even if all I wanted was to run away in general, with no particular place to go, even that would be difficult. All day long Mr. Goat watches me with one steely eye. If he lets up for one minute, Rolf hauls himself up and walks stiff-legged over to wherever I am, plops himself down, and trains his yellow eyes on me.

"Behold!" Svaalberd shouts in a voice like a parson's, startling me out of my reverie. "Away from the fatness of the earth shall your dwelling be, and away from the dew of heaven on high, and thou shalt . . ."

I lose track of his preaching and start pondering just what he's got that's so precious he has to lock it up. Or is he just a miserly old man who so treasures his moldy cheese and weevil-infested grain that he fears the likes of me?

". . . fill the wood box, clean the fireplace," Svaalberd goes on, "scrub out the copper kettles—till they shine, mind you!" By now I've figured out that he has laid off scripture and has moved on to my list of chores. ". . . I'll be expecting supper when I get home, too." He shuts the Bible with a thump and finishes by saying, "Genesis twenty-seven and twenty-eight. Amen."

The Bible goes back in the chest, where it is locked away with a rattle and a clank. Then he hoists himself out of his chair and takes his ring of keys out to the storehouse. After a while he comes by again, this time with two big bags. With these slung over his shoulder, he proceeds away down the mountainside.

"Bring me a pair of shoes!" I holler after him. "Or a golden wreath!"

But he's too far away or else pretending not to hear me.

As soon as he's gone, I run to the storehouse myself. It's a far piece from the house, all uphill. Why he built the little building so far away, I don't know, and by the time I get to it, my heart is beating hard. I stop and press my ear to the door. It seems, for a moment . . . a sound. Then, nothing. I try the latch again. But of course, the door is locked. He's probably said a charm over it.

It seems the goatman has a charm and a spell for everything. To keep the fire burning and to quench it, to stanch blood, to ward against fever and snakebite.

You can bet I pay close attention when he mumbles these things, and I've been learning a thing or two. To turn back a wasp you have only to say, "Brown man! Brown man in the bush! Sting stick and stone but not Christian man's flesh and bone!" If you need still more, recite the Lord's Prayer.

I'll thank you to keep that to yourself.

❧❧❧

As the sun is setting, here the goatman comes, back up the mountain with the same two sacks, looking just as full as they did going down. Up to the storehouse he goes and then back down to the house.

"How is it you had all day and still didn't clean the ashes out of the fireplace?" he asks when he comes in.

It seems the only thing he brought me is a cross word.

I n the story of the white bear, one night the girl got up and, when she heard the bear sleeping, struck a match and lit a candle. When the light shone upon him, she saw that he was not a bear but the loveliest prince anyone ever set eyes on!

So this night I decide to look, to see if anything similar happens to the goatman. I creep out of bed and toss Rolf a crust of bread to keep him quiet. There are still enough embers in the fire to light a candle, and so I take the pathetic stub of candle that Svaalberd allows me, get a little flame burning, and steal quietly to his bed, holding the light as near to him as I dare. My heart is pounding. What if? I think. What if he has turned into a beautiful man? What then?

I lean over, closer and closer, and just like in the story, a drop of hot tallow from the candle drips onto his shirt.

"What the devil?" the goatman yelps, jumping up. "What are you doing, girl?"

Of course I have nothing to say to that.

"Lonely, are you? Is that it? Come looking for companion-ship?" He reaches out toward me, and I slap his hand away.

"Don't touch me," I growl, using the tone I learned from his own dog. I snap my teeth, too, and run to my bed—hearing his hoarse breathing behind me. Then I feel his arms wrap around my waist, and he throws me down on my bed, me face-down and him on top of me.

"Foolish man!" I cry. "You've forgotten something!"

"What's that?" he says, his foul breath on my neck.

With my hand under the pillow, I feel the knife handle and curl my fingers around it. In one swift movement, I pull it out and twist around to face him, placing the blade against his neck.

His eyes bulge, and the big vein on his neck stands out, pulsing and pulsing. Just the slightest push from me will slice it clear through.

Straw into Gold

Rolf whines, and the goatman grunts and stands up, moving away from the knife.

He doesn't reproach or threaten me as I expect. He says, "Come summer, we will go down to the church and have the parson marry us. Then I'll take you to my bed."

"One of us will go to hell first," I mumble.

"What's that?" he says, spinning around. He grabs my arm; the knife clatters to the floor. He yanks me out of bed and pushes me out of the house.

"You're a danger to me and to my peace of mind," he grumbles as he hustles me across the farmyard. "I won't have a murderess in the house, waiting till I sleep to slit my throat—"

"I never did! You were the one who threatened—"

"You're a girl who can't be trusted, I can see that, all right!" he squawks, dragging me up the hill. He's rattling the keys, turning the lock on the storehouse door, and then I'm inside, shivering in my shift. The door is slammed, a key is turned, and with a click I am locked inside.

"Here is the place for girls who can't be trusted!" he yells from outside the door, then stomps away.

I'll sit right here on the step and weep, I will. I mean to, but I hear something—the same sound I heard once in the quiet of the night. A whirr. A hum. Coming from somewhere nearby. From inside this building.

✳✳✳✳

Up the dark stairs I go. With each step the sound grows louder and the darkness less dark.

The sound is both familiar and unfamiliar—as if I've heard it a thousand times before, but never quite like this. It makes a kind of strange music, almost. It calls back memories the way certain smells do, like the way crushed cardamom makes a smell like Christmas.

At the top of the stairs, I stand and gape. Candlelight illuminates the loft—a room meant for storing food, and there is plenty here: Smoked meats and sausages hang from the rafters; there are stacks of flatbread and barrels of barley and rye. There's a heap of sheepskins, too, and piles of wool.

But it isn't this that makes me stare. It's that, in the midst of all this, there is a spinning wheel purring away, and at the spinning wheel sits a girl. Or what looks like a girl, all surrounded by the glow of candlelight.

"*Hei!*" I say.

She looks up at me but says nothing.

"Who are you?" I ask.

No answer.

"What's your name?"

Still no answer.

"How long have you been sitting here, spinning?"

Nothing.

"Are you deaf?" I ask. "DEAF?" I shout.

No answer.

"Maybe you're just rude!"

No response.

A strange-looking creature she is: small but soft and round as rising bread dough, and her hands like white sweet rolls, spinning wool. How old might she be? She looks on the one hand like a child, on the other like a very old woman. She's a strange one, so silent and unspeaking, with her wide gray eyes and her soft face.

She knows how to spin, there's no denying that. On the floor to one side of her is a heap of wool, and on the other side is a pile of well-spun yarn, smooth and perfect, all neatly looped into skeins.

"That's very fine yarn you've made," I tell her.

Maybe there's the hint of a smile, although it might be just the way the candlelight flickers along her face.

Deep into the night she sits and spins, her wheel purring like a contented cat. While she spins yarn, I spin yarns. I tell her stories of Soria Moria, and the castle that lies east of the sun and west of the moon.

I tell her how I made the same mistake as the girl in the story who dropped tallow on the bear-prince's shirt. "Do you know that story?" I ask the spinning girl. "And how the prince woke and said, 'What have you done? Now you have made us both unhappy forever. If you had only held out one year I should have been saved. I have been bewitched to be a bear by day and a man by night. But now all is over between us, and I must go to the castle that lies east of the sun and west of the moon, where I will have to marry the troll princess with a nose three ells long.'"

I tell the spinning girl that I tried the same thing with the candle, and everything happened just like in the story, except that it turns out old Goatbeard is just as goaty and trollish in sleep as he is in daylight. "And it begins to seem that you and I are princesses," I tell her, "held captive by the old troll himself!" I am being more than nice to call her a princess, for she looks nothing at all like any princess you might imagine. But then neither do I, I suppose.

"In the stories," I go on, "someone always comes to rescue the princesses. A prince or even a simple boy in raggedy clothes with a spot of soot on his nose. And so shall someone rescue us, I shouldn't wonder."

That's what I tell her, but as her wheel whirs, my mind whirs along with it, and soon I've run out of golden thread with which to spin my pretty stories and I'm left with just the thin thread of truth. And that wiry, rough little thread tells me that if anyone is going to do any rescuing from this place, it's going to have to be me.

Winter

Something is different. As soon as I open my eyes, I can tell. The tiny square of light coming in the one grubby window has changed; it isn't yellow-gold anymore. This light is a pale gray-blue, like milk without the cream mixed in. I know before I look outside: It has snowed.

The door bangs open, and I hear the stomp of the goatman's boots, then catch the whiff of the cold outdoors, of snow wetting down his woolen jacket.

"Get up, you lazy wench. The work doesn't end because it snows. The goats need feeding."

I get up and pull on the clothes and shoes he tosses me, then stomp out to the goat shed.

It must have snowed all night long; it's knee-deep and still coming down. I'm trudging through it when I notice Svaal-berd leading Snowflake right into the house.

"What kind of madness is this? Girls sleep in the store-house while the goats go in the house?" I ask.

"She's about to give birth, and I don't want to risk the kid freezing outside," he says. "Fetch some straw and bring it in here."

28

I retrieve some straw, bring it in, and strew it around.

"Who's that girl in the storehouse?" I ask him as he pats Snowflake's heavy belly.

"This is what comes of her getting out when she shouldn't!" he exclaims.

"Who?"

"Snowflake!"

"I'm asking of the *girl*. Who is she?"

"She didn't say anything to you, I don't suppose?" the goatman asks me.

"Why?" I ask back.

"Well, did she?" His eyes shift here and there while he pretends to busy himself with Snowflake.

"You must know yourself if she talks or doesn't," I say.

"Nary a word to me," he says.

"Nor to me," say I.

He nods, pleased, and gives Snowflake a satisfied smack.

"Well?" I persist. "What about her?"

"She'll be having twins, I shouldn't doubt."

"The girl?"

"No, Snowflake!" he says.

"I'm asking of the girl," I remind him.

"Found her when she was just a babe, crawling about on all fours out in the wild, all alone. Seems her people just threw her away. Thought she was a changeling, most like," he says.

Changeling! A sudden chill passes through my sweater and makes me shiver.

"Left for the trolls to take, I shouldn't wonder. But it seems even the trolls didn't want her!" He laughs at this, and then goes on. "So I took her. Turned out she wasn't much of a worker. Too slow to be much good at anything. But once she found spinning, well! When it comes to spinning, there's not her like to be found."

"Is she happy at that work, then?" I ask.

"Why, if she isn't, she ought to be!" is his answer. "She's got it better than she should."

Snowflake bleats and cries. She tries to lie down, then stands, then tries to lie down again. Oh, but Svaalberd is all gentleness, speaking kindnesses to her like he never has to me.

"Good girl," he says, as she begins to bear down, pushing and bleating by turns. She seems to be having a time of it, but after a bit something starts to appear.

"There's a leg," I say.

The goatman turns to me and says, "Why do you stand there, useless? Build up the fire some!"

I throw more wood on the fire, while peppering him with questions about the spinning girl. He says that the girl never uttered a sound, on account of her mother getting too close to an elder tree before she was born, he reckons.

"Why do you keep her locked up like that?" I ask.

"For her own safety, that's why. She might wander off and get lost! She could get hurt."

The baby goat lands with a plop on the straw, and Svaalberd says, proud as a papa, "There's the kid! A doe."

Snowflake turns around and starts in cleaning up the tiny creature, sweet as can be, with its floppy ears too big for the rest of it.

"Anyway, she's got strange powers, that one," the goatman says.

"Snowflake?" I ask, over her cries. She's bleating and pushing again.

"No, the girl," says the goatman. "You don't want her too near the does' shed, or they may stop giving milk. And you don't see me shaving, do you? No, you don't. For should the girl get hold of my whiskers, she could make a potion with them and cast a spell to weaken and sicken me."

I look at his scraggly beard and think, I would not want to touch those whiskers, even if I could make a potion out of them.

"Do you really believe that?" I say. "The parson says we're not to hold to such things—superstitions and the like. And when it comes to matters of health, we should put our faith in the doctor."

"Doctor!" Svaalberd scoffs. "When have you ever seen one of those in these parts?" Just as he says this, out comes another kid, *plop!* onto the straw.

"Twins, it is," Svaalberd exclaims, then, "Ohhh . . ." His tone changes, and I look up from my bellows work, for the fire seems all smoke and nothing else today.

He *tsk*s and clucks and shakes his shaggy head. "Take this one out, and put it in the snow."

I study the second kid, small as a kitten and unsteady. He rocks on his little pegs trying to stand, and his funny ears flop from side to side. "He isn't dead," I say. "And look: Snowflake is cleaning him up, too. She's not rejected him."

"He'll never grow up right," Svaalberd says. "So there's no point in feeding him."

"It's only his leg is a little funny," I suggest.

"Nay," the goatman says. "Best to get it over now."

"But—" I start.

"Maybe you'd like to go fetch the *doctor*!" he snaps and shows me the back of his hand. "Now take him out."

"Do it yourself," I tell him, turning back to poke at the fire. "I don't care if you slap me. I won't do it."

When I look over my shoulder, there is just the one kid, and Snowflake staring at the door. If I didn't like old Goatbeard before, now where he is concerned, my heart has hardened into black coal.

The Ash Lad

So our life goes on. Snowflake and her kid in the house with Svaalberd, and me in the storehouse with Spinning Girl. Luckily there's a stove in there. So I've got both stove and fireplace for which to chop kindling, to carry wood, to stoke and to tend.

At first, I keep my eye on the girl, wondering if she's human or what. Could she be a *hulder*-maid—one of the invisibles, as Svaalberd said? Her work seems to go from dusk until dawn, as they say the *huldrefolks'* does.

"Who are you?" I ask her, and "From whence do you come?" and even "Are you a human girl, or what?"

What *is* it, I wonder, that makes us human?

"Turn around one time," I tell her, and she does. There's no tail poking out from under her skirt. She's not hollowed out from behind, either, as they say *huldre*-maids are.

"Sometimes I feel like a *hulder*-maid myself," I say, "for there are times when I feel as hollow as a lightning-struck tree trunk." There are times, too, when I feel as invisible as air.

Human or no, Spinning Girl and I get used to each other. She soon comes after my hair as if it's a pile of dirty wool, picking the sticks, twigs, dirt, and thistles out of it, then braiding it or twisting it into fancy plaits.

That's in the eventide. Workdays, I go through my chores, trying to stop wishing I could get away. Because running away is impossible now that winter is here. The snow stays and winter stays, and I stay.

Some people think it's a romantic job to tend the goats, for they picture the goat girl up in the mountain *seter* when it's summer and the sun is in the sky all the time. The grass is thick and green and the sun warm on your face, and nothing to do all day but braid wildflowers into wreaths and gather cloudberries. Those people forget about winter.

Then it's wake up in the dark, eat breakfast in the dark, haul feed in the dark, gather forage in the dark, cut fir boughs in the dark, haul water in the dark. Oh, and shovel the snow and chop the wood and haul the wood and clean out the ashes and start the fire and rake the coals and cook the porridge and make the candles and knead the bread. All in the dark, dark, dark.

The sun, if there is any at all, never gets above the trees, so you only imagine it. The best you can hope for is to see its pale, cold light winking between the branches. All the while your hands are frozen, red, and cracked. You have to blow on them to get your fingers to bend. And your shoes are always full of snow because your master is too mean to buy you a pair of boots.

The days and weeks go by, and by, and by. The snow is

melting; the sun is getting higher in the sky; the goats drop their kids, and they're all let out to find some grass. Still, I barely notice any of it, since all I know is milking goats, making cheese, hauling buckets, all accompanied by a kick or a slap or a tug on my braids.

⊁⊁⊱⊰⊰

*Y*ank. "Girl, why haven't you covered the milk?" The goat-man points to the buckets lined up next to me.

"I'm still milking."

"Keep your tongue in your mouth," he says.

I shrug. *Slap to the back of the head.* "You cover them pails," he says. "Keep the dirt out."

I turn slowly to stare at him. This is the man who hasn't bathed since King Olaf challenged the gods of Dale-Gudbrand.

"You don't bathe," I say. "Your house isn't fit for pigs to live in. The barn was full of goat dung until I came and cleaned it up. You haven't let me wash my hair the whole time I've been here. And you're worried that a dust mote might alight on the cream?"

I feel a hand yank my arm and lift me up, then my heels dragging in the dirt. I can see the hand coming at my face, and although I turn away at the last minute, the blow lands on my cheek. A sharp sting followed by an ache that will blossom into a purple bruise, I'm sure. A few more of those, and I lose count. I run my tongue along my teeth to see if they're all still there,

35

but my lips are already puffy and swollen, my mouth full of something I suppose is blood.

I'm tossed down into the yard, which is a mud hole from the spring thaw. So first I feel cold muck seeping through my dress, and next I feel something wet slosh over me. At first I think—hope—I'm under the pump and he's pumping cold water over me, but this liquid comes at me from a bucket. It's warm and sticky and stinks like Odin's underdrawers.

"And by the way, that is *your* job—emptying the chamber pot," the goatman says. "And since you didn't, that's what you deserve, you filthy-mouthed little wench." Off he stomps to the house, muttering.

Mud-caked, bloody, and stinking, I stand up and am about to scrape some of the filth off me when something catches my eye. Something different, something that doesn't belong.

It couldn't be a person. Not a single person has come by in all the long months I've been here—including, I think bitterly, any of my relatives. And sadly, Greta, who I know would have come had she been allowed to travel by herself. But of course she is only eight years old and too young for that.

Is it an animal? A tree suddenly burst into leaves? Or a *hulder* caught out in broad daylight? No, it's a human being, with a corona of light around his head, so it could only be a saint or maybe the crown prince. Oh, sure, the crown prince *would* come visiting when I'm in worse condition than a pig.

When he steps forward, I see that it isn't the crown prince, just a boy, not so much older than me, with a pack upon his back. He stands under a birch tree that has come out in catkins all lit up from the sun behind them—as is the boy's yellow hair. That is what makes the halo. A swarm of spring midges enhances the effect.

I must be gaping, for he says so, adding, "Your master, miss?"

I'm sure I've never heard a more honeyed voice, and I open my mouth to reply, but my mouth being swollen—a tooth or two broken, likely—only garble comes out.

"Poor soul," the boy mutters and begins to make his way toward the house, giving me a wide berth.

The goatman comes out and calls to me. *"Mus!"* he says. "Catch Snowflake and put her back in the pen. Then finish that milking you didn't get done."

Sure enough, Snowflake is out nibbling at the lower branches of the firs. I go after her while trying to keep my eye on the boy and my master. Svaalberd points off into the distance as if he's giving directions, while the boy nods and shields his eyes against the sun to look. So he's lost, which explains how he got here. The two of them go inside the house. What else are they talking about? I wonder. As soon as I get Snowflake in the shed, I run to the house and stand in the doorway, listening.

". . . thought she was a changeling, you know," the goatman's saying as he wraps up a hunk of cheese. "Her kin tried all kinds of remedies: They flogged her three Thursdays in a row, threatened to put her in the fire, and finally threw her out. I found her crawling about the forest on all fours, took pity on her, and brought her here. Her own people wanted naught to do with her."

At first I think he's talking about Spinning Girl, but then he says, "Covers herself in dung every day. Try as I might, she won't keep herself clean—" and I realize he's talking about *me*.

This makes me so mad, I fly into the house with my nails toward Svaalberd's eyeballs. Of course, he subdues me and nods his head in a pitying way. He hands the parcel of cheese and bread to the boy, and the boy gives him a coin. (And though it's the bread and cheese *I* made, am I likely to ever see that coin? No.)

"Done my best to raise her up Christian, but as you can see, she's little but a wild bear herself. You see how she injures herself," he says, clucking his tongue and touching—a little too hard—my tender bruises. "She runs into things, falls. Who knows how these things happen?"

"For the love of God!" I cry. "What a liar you are!" But my lips are so swollen it comes out sounding like my mouth is full of porridge.

"Never learned to talk properly, either, poor girl."

I kick him in the shins, and he winces. For a moment I

think his temper will win and he'll smack me, which he surely would do if the boy weren't here.

For the boy, old Goatbeard manages the kind of smile the devil might use if he were trying to impersonate the baby Jesus in the manger. It makes me want to vomit. Or perhaps that's from all the blood I've swallowed, and suddenly I have to run outside and empty my stomach over the fence.

Naturally, that's when the handsome fellow steps out of the house. Mr. Goat follows, shaking his head as if with concern for my immortal soul.

"Many thanks for setting me back on the proper course," the boy says. "I'll be on my way . . ." My heart sinks. Even one night might give my injuries enough time to heal so I could speak to him. "Off to America," he finishes.

I look up. America? A thousand questions crowd my mind. How are you getting there? Which direction is it? How much money do you need for a venture like that? Do you know my father?

Instead of any of those, I manage, with great care, to form a nearly coherent sentence: "I want to go with you."

The boy turns to me, looking at me as if for the first time.

"Aye." Mr. Goat nods, his eyes shifting uneasily. "From time to time she comes out with something that sounds as if it makes perfect sense, poor thing."

I resist with all my might throwing a clod of dirt at him.

I'll pay enough as it is. And he'll only twist my actions to make me seem more dull-witted.

"Our ship will be sailing within a fortnight. I'm to be meeting my kin there, so I'd best be off," the boy says, shouldering his pack, already moving away. Already just a bright spot moving among the dark pines.

When the boy is just about to disappear over the rise, I make my move, bolting for the edge of the farmyard. I can hear the goatman chasing me, breathing hard, and then, oh! his paws clutching. He claps his hand over my mouth, and while I twist and struggle, he kicks open the door to the storehouse. With a shove I am inside, the door slams shut, and the lock turns with a hard metallic *clank* that seems to ring inside me.

I won't sink down right here and weep. Oh, no. I won't give him the satisfaction. Instead, I dash right up the steps to the loft and stand at the window that faces out over the valley, where I can watch the blond head flickering like sunshine among the birches.

The sun is ahead of him now; he is walking west. *West.* That is the direction I will have to go to get to America.

Spinning Girl presses a damp rag to my face and wipes the blood and filth from my limbs. When I'm as clean as I'm going to get, she goes back to her work. As she spins her yarn, I spin a golden dream out of dust motes. A dream of going to America.

To the *Seter*

he next morning, the goatman shouts from outside the storehouse. "Up, you worthless girl. It's time to take the goats up the mountain to the *seter*."

He stands outside with a jacket over his arm and a walking staff in his hand.

"It looks to me as if you're taking them yourself," I say.

"Just showing you how to get there," he answers.

"If you point in the general direction," I tell him, "I'll find it."

"Wouldn't it be fine if it were so simple as that?" he says.

"What about the spinning girl?" I ask. "What is she going to do?"

"That's no concern of yours," he says, striking off with such a stride that I have to run to keep up.

Then I remember something. "You told the boy I was a changeling. That's the same story you told me about the girl in the loft."

"Maybe it was you; maybe it was her," he says. "It was one of you—who's to know which one?"

"What do you mean by that?" I ask him.

He stops for a moment, turns back to me, and eyes me up and down. "By looks, I'd say it was her. But by temperament, I'd say it was you."

Before I can ask any more about that, he charges up and over a hill.

Through a grove of stunted birches we go, then through tall timber, their trunks twisted by the wind. Here and there a little patch of snow. After a while I start to wonder just where we are going. Our way seems to lead more down than up.

The goatman prattles on about jobs for me to do once I'm at the *seter*, while pointing out the plants and herbs growing along the way. "You must get up on the roof and pull out the saplings that have started to grow in the sod. While you're up there, clean out the chimney. Here's yarrow, good to stanch bleeding. You've also got to oil the leather hinges and grease the latches."

I think of the ship that's leaving in less than a fortnight. If I can get away from the goatman and find my way back to Greta, maybe we could get to the ship in time. But what will we do for money? I don't suppose they'll let us on the ship for nothing! And then there's the issue of just where we are now compared with where that ship is.

We come out of the trees into an open meadow, bright with new spring grass, and I forget about all these troubles. Glittering mountain peaks surround us, from which silvery waterfalls tumble down. Streams are moving again and chatter along over stones. The smell of the new grass, of growing things, of warm earth and running water—all of it smells of possibility. This is what America smells like, I think.

Why, it makes me want to sing!

"'This king, I must tell, was out of his head,'" I sing. "'His child by trolls had been taken. And troll king and princess soon would be wed—'"

"You shouldn't be singing of trolls," Svaalberd barks. "Not here."

"Why?"

"''Tis said they live hereabouts," he says.

"Do you really believe in all that?" I ask him. "You, a Christian man and all?"

"You're the one singing about them," he says.

"Just because I sing a song about them doesn't mean I believe in them," I tell him.

"Well, if you don't, you ought to," he mumbles.

"The parson says we're not to continue believing in trolls and such," I say. "And furthermore, we're not to be relying on spells and charms. It shows a disrespect for God, he says." That part is hard to believe, for it seems to me that most folks in these parts believe so fervently in God that scarcely a charm can be spoken without saying the Lord's Prayer or invoking the Holy Trinity. Why, a charm is really useless without it.

43

"If you want to sing, you should sing a hymn," the goatman says, starting in: "'The world is very evil, the times are waxing late. Be sober and keep vigil, the Judge is at the gate . . .'"

My jaw drops, because his singing voice hardly matches anything else about him. It is low and melodious, quite a pleasure to hear. "You should sing more often," I say, when he's finished his verse.

He smiles and comes toward me like he means to kiss me! You can be sure I scramble away as fast as ever I can, so I am out of breath when we stop at the edge of a river, rushing with melting ice. The jingle of the goats' bells can barely be heard over the noise of it.

"Here we cross," says Svaalberd.

"Where's the bridge?" I ask.

"There isn't one."

"How are we supposed to get across?"

"Walk or swim."

"I hope you're jesting," I say. The water is as cold as the snow and ice that it so recently was. Its swift current could pull you down as fast as any water sprite. "What about the goats?"

"The goats can swim."

"Well, I can't."

"I'll carry you across the river," says he.

The thought of letting old Goatbeard carry me—in any way or for any reason whatsoever—turns my stomach.

"How is it we're so far down in the valley?" I ask him. "It seems we've gone more down than up. Shouldn't we be climbing *up* the mountain to get to the *seter*?"

"I thought we might as well go to the church first and get married. And then you can go on up to the *seter*."

Marry! "I don't remember saying I would marry you," I protest.

"You have to marry someone," he says.

If I could think of one of his curses, I'd lay it on him right now. Instead, I say, "Well, look. You cross the river first."

"It's shallow," he says.

"I don't believe it," I insist.

"Well, it is."

"It doesn't look shallow."

"Well, it is."

"Prove it. You go across and let me watch."

"Hold my jacket," he says, handing me the jacket he's been carrying over his arm.

I take it and glance quickly at the goats, who all have their heads down, munching grass. All except Daisy, who is busy biting the ears of the kids.

Svaalberd spits and makes the sign of the cross. "Trolls in the depths," he says. "See! The sign of the cross. Keep away—I belong to God!"

The devil you do, I think, but I keep my mouth shut, and

he wades into the water. The water is glacial blue foamed into almost white. Who knows what sorcery might lie beneath?

Rolf plunges in after him and commences to swim. The goats look up from their munching to eyeball Svaalberd, then turn their heads toward me. They don't want to cross that river either and will wait for me before they do anything.

Svaalberd has to pick his way along the stones and boulders littering the river bottom, which he can't see but can feel with his feet. That and the rushing current naturally make for slow going. But I can see the water never gets higher than his waist.

Midway, he stops, turns, and calls back to me. "See?" He stretches his arms to show—well, what? That they are still above water, I suppose.

"Go all the way across," I call out. "It could still get deeper."

He slowly plows his way across the river. His shirt gets wet, and I can see the muscles in his back ripple and flex. Except for the hump, which I have long since gotten used to, his back from here looks like a young man's!

I squint. Does he look better because he is so far away, and there is a barrier between us? Or has some kind of bewitchery happened to him in the river?

I think of a story my uncle told of a man on this mountain slope who'd seen a *hulder*-maid from across a river. She was beautiful, and the man hadn't noticed the tail poking out from under her skirt. He was fooled into marrying her, as it happens. Somehow, though, he'd gotten out of the marriage yet still ended up with a treasure of troll gold and some magic of his own.

Could the stories be true? I wonder.

A sudden vivid memory of those two coins on Uncle's table rushes back to me—how had the goatman come by those? Why had I never wondered about this before? Why does he keep everything locked up tight when nary a soul passes by?

What if . . . I begin to wonder . . . What if the old goat has a treasure hidden somewhere on his property? A hoard of gold?

Svaalberd climbs up the far bank and stands to his full height, which from this distance looks reasonable. He doesn't look so stooped.

Of this man who'd gotten a troll treasure, much was whispered. He'd had a wife long ago when he was young, so it was said. A human wife. She'd been a *kloke kone*—a wisewoman, a healer—who helped the neighbors with births and burns and knew all manner of cures. Still, for all that, she had been unable to save herself when she became ill, and so she died. The man, it was said, had removed himself from the company of people and had gone up in the mountains to farm some bit of rocky ground.

"Come on!" he shouts. "You can make it easily. My legs are

numb with cold. I don't want to wade back for you now . . ." He shouts on and on. I stop listening and let the rush of the water and the roar of excitement fill my ears.

I have become aware of something heavy in one of the goatman's jacket pockets. My hand slips into the pocket and my fingers feel the keys—his big ring of keys. The ring goes into my hand, and I drop the jacket, then turn and bolt, running as fast as I can up and down the steep hillside, my heart pounding. The goats' bells *cling clang*, and their hooves clatter as they follow behind me. Stones skitter under my feet and *ping* down the slope as I race and run, now slipping, now hopping, now skidding, now running, my thumping feet pounding out the words: *treasure treasure treasure.*

Treasure

Past the bright patches of snow, into the tall pines through the twisted birches, back into the pasture, and finally I run full bore into the farmyard and stop. How odd, how still, how quiet it is. A stream of sunlight makes its crooked way through the trees. It seems so gentle—empty, the whole place sweeter. Pleasant, even. But I have no time to think of that. I have to find the treasure.

Treasure! The word has pounded itself into my brain on the long run back to the farm. First, the storeroom, for which I now have the key.

The key in the lock, the latch unlatched, and I am inside, turning over crates, peeking inside barrels, kicking over old planks. Sausages, cheese, old potatoes, and my own little bundle of things—all these things get stuffed into a gunnysack.

Spinning Girl sits staring at me as I do this, and a part of me knows that I haven't properly thought of what to do about her.

"Girl," I say to her, "this is your chance to make your escape. What do you want to do?"

No answer.

Perhaps she has her own plan, I think, which doesn't involve me.

A dog barks. From afar, but they're coming, dog and master.

I dash into the yard, and from there into the house. Straightaway, my eyes alight upon Svaalberd's locked chest.

"There are some fine things in that chest, I shouldn't wonder," I say, crossing quickly to it, fumbling with the ring of keys until I find the right one. The lock clicks; the lid opens. There is the Bible, and next to it a leather pouch. *Clinkity jingle* it goes when I pick it up. It takes but one peek to see what is inside: coins. Many coins.

To take them would be stealing.

But if it's troll's treasure? Is it a sin to steal what's already stolen? Stolen thrice: once from humans by trolls, then from the trolls by the goatman. And finally—I stuff the bag of coins in the gunnysack—stolen from the goatman by me.

I touch the Bible, but I won't take it. *That* would be a sin.

Still, I lift it up. There's a sheaf of papers, and beneath that, more papers. I leaf through them, words on paper, keep looking. And then I see it—what the goatman must have been talking about. His book of charms and cures and spells: the Black Book.

I stare at its smudged black cover, but I don't pick it up— oh, no! It might burn my fingers! I leave that book where it lies, replace the papers, place the Bible back on top, and slam the lid down. Moving past the table, I take the wide-bladed knife, slide it into the sack, and out I go, blinking, into the daylight.

But, oh! Svaalberd is right there, just coming around the side of the storehouse, turning to notice the door of it hanging open.

Quick! His back is turned, and I dash across the yard and duck into the goat shed. But how can I get out without him seeing me? I think of Snowflake, and how she escapes. And how Svaalberd never did discover how she does it. But *I* know. And the forest edge is right there, right outside that busted board.

The dog's hoarse cry grows closer.

Keeping my eyes on the shed door, I back into the nanny's stall. A soft sound makes me turn, and it's all I can do to stifle a scream. There's Spinning Girl, hunkered in the shadows.

Rolf's toenails click against the hard-packed dirt in the shed.

I look at the girl, her gray eyes suddenly lit with fear, and push her toward the board that leads to freedom. Behind me, the dog woofs a cheery greeting at me.

"Go away, Rolf!" I growl.

But he snuffles around outside the stall door, panting and whining, and now yelping, and that'll raise the master! My shushing is to no avail. A punch in the snout would just set him to howling.

I could take out the knife and silence the dog with a lunging stab, make the barking stop. Once the dog was still, I could cover it with straw. It would take Mr. Goat some time, looking all over. Time enough for me to slip out under the broken board. I should do it if I'm going to. I should do it now.

But I can't. Instead, I pull the sausages out of the gunnysack and shove them under the door. The dog drags them away, disappearing into a corner.

But it's too late, isn't it? The goatman is already in the shed. His footsteps grow closer.

The Ring of Keys

I scoot to the wall, pulling the girl with me. Gingerly, I raise the busted board and push her through. Not so easy, as she is round and the opening is square. But there, now she's out, and it's my turn. My head is out; I smell the spring air!

But, ah! A hand clamps around my leg. Out of the corner of my eye I see the girl waddling away into the forest while Svaalberd drags me, kicking and wiggling, out of the shed and into the house. I get plunked in a chair, and the sack is overturned and all the contents roll and clatter onto the kitchen table. The cheese and bits of broken flatbread and old potatoes, and of course the coins come out, *clinkity clink*, and the knife clunks out, and my own little bundle falls out and comes undone, and finally, even Mama's brooch lands with a polite little clatter on the tabletop.

Mr. Goat looks up at me. The corner of one eye twitches, and the vein in his neck pulses. "I see what kind of plotting you've been up to when you were pretending to work." He grunts and spits as he drags the unlocked chest over to the table. "Your people led me to believe that in spite of all, you were a good girl, a trustworthy girl, and here I find you stealing from the master and about to run away." He *tsk-tsk*s and runs his tongue along his snaggleteeth.

All the while, he's pinching up the coins and popping them into the box. I follow his eyes as they dart to the brooch. They gleam, as if to say, "Now there's a pretty bit of finery!"

When I see his hand inching toward it, his fingers reaching for it, my heart leaps into my mouth, and the knife leaps into my hand. My hand rises up over my head, and in one unflinching moment, the heavy blade comes down—down upon the goatman's hands—and when the blade is raised, two of his fingers are gone.

Let me tell you, old Goatbeard is none too happy about it. He hops up and screams, staring wild-eyed at his hand, at the blood pumping out.

I hop up, too; the wooden box is opened, and everything he's tossed into it seems to leap up and fling itself back into the gunnysack: every coin, every bit of food, every crumb on the table. Out of the expanding pool of blood, I pluck my mother's brooch. The fingers I leave behind.

"Stand still, blood!" the man chants, speaking to his bloody stumps. "I bid you stop as surely as one is forbidden heaven's door..."

I know where he gets all his spells and magic. If I had the book he's got—though most likely it was his wife's book to start, and it was she who taught him all these charms—if I had that book, I might well have all that magic myself. Although, by the look of it, his blood-stopping charm isn't working. Still, he chants on, ". . . stand still, blood, not one drop more. In the name of three . . ."

Back to the chest I go and reach down under the Bible and the papers, saying to myself, "Now that I've done what I've done, it hardly matters what else I may do." I pluck that Black Book with its stained cover and thumbed and dirty pages, pluck it out of the box and take it.

The goatman notices me as if for the first time. Now he points at me with his good hand. With burning eyes and trembling finger, he says, "At the cost of your soul! Take it at the cost of your soul!"

Then out the door I dash and make straight for the birches. Maybe my nose can follow the clean, soapy scent of the yellow-haired boy who'd traveled this way.

Svaalberd howls. "I conjure you, devils in heaven and on earth, to stop the person who has stolen from me." His curses follow me as I run and run, headed west. "Do not allow this person tranquility or rest, neither sleeping nor waking . . ."

If I don't hear the curse, maybe it can't hurt me?

". . . sitting nor lying, walking nor standing, riding nor driving . . ."

Down and down and down I run. Svaalberd's voice follows me: "Thus I throw this curse on her, that she will never have rest on this earth . . ."

Eventually I will come to a road. Or if not a road, a trail. Or if not a trail, a cow path. Anything that will lead me some-where—away.

"What are you doing?" the globeflowers seem to ask, nodding their yellow heads at me. "Where are you going?" the darting catchflies say. And the aspen leaves just *tsk tsk tsk,* turning in the wind.

Oh! Greta! I have to go get her, and I have to get there be-fore the goatman does. For, once his fingers are bound and the pain subsides, old Svaalberd will head for Aunt and Uncle's. Once there, he'll demand restitution for all that he's lost—his money, his fingers—and punishment for the crime committed.

"What's gone is gone," Aunt will say, meaning she already spent the money he gave her and has no more. "And besides, Astri is not here, and there's no use crying over the loss of her."

What will he say to that? He'll say, "I want another girl, then."

But Aunt won't give up one of her own girls. She'll sug-gest that he take the youngest—Greta.

The thought of it cuts into me. I might as well have swung that knife back on myself and started sawing a hole in my chest through which to pull out my own heart.

I will have to get there first, ahead of the goatman, and get Greta away.

But how? I don't know where Aunt and Uncle live!

Why, oh, why didn't I pay attention when Mr. Goat led me away that first night? I could have at least noticed if I was going up mountains or down dales. Were there streams to cross? Forests to walk through? Now I don't know where to go, and yet somehow I have to get there before the goatman does.

But what if . . . what if the goatman and I get there *at the same time*?

I turn and climb back up the mountainside. My legs burn. My lungs burn. My head spins. But I don't stop until I reach the fringe of woods below the goat farm. There I stop, hands on knees, breathing hard.

The farm is quiet. Flies buzz in that peculiar way they do when they think they're alone, with no one to pester. Rolf, stuffed with his recent meal, lies sprawled in the sun, fast asleep. This tranquil scene reminds me with a pang that I could have spent the summer at the *seter*. How lovely it would have been to spend every gloriously long day up high on the mountain, alone. I would have lolled about in the warm heather, weaving myself crowns of wildflowers. I would have been the princess of my domain, in my kingdom of goats. And none of this horror would have happened.

I am deep in reminiscence of what never was when old

Goatbeard comes out of the house and limps toward the shed. Why a couple of missing fingers would make him limp, I do not know, but limp he does, gathering up the goats and urging them into the shed with a switch.

Then out of the shed he comes, muttering. He swings his head from side to side as if looking for something. Into the house and out again, tells the dog to stay, and finally sets off with his walking staff and flask.

I am just sneaking after him when I see her—Spinning Girl, standing among the trees on the far side of the farmyard, as if she has been waiting for me there all this time. In her hand, glinting in the sun, is Svaalberd's ring of keys.

Red as Blood, White as Snow

It's slow going with Spinning Girl. She doesn't so much walk as waddle, tipping from one side to the other, and every step is a huff and a puff. So it isn't long before we lose sight of the goatman. Finally, there's nothing to be done but to stop.

We sit down on a sun-warmed stone and pluck at tufts of bog cotton.

"Once, there was a queen," I begin, by way of explaining our predicament, "whose nose began to bleed. As she looked at the red blood on the white snow, she said, 'If I had a daughter as white as snow and red as blood, it wouldn't matter at all about my sons.' The next thing she knew, she had a daughter, but her twelve sons turned into wild ducks and flew away."

I look at Spinning Girl. "Maybe you were bewitched like that," I muse. "If there was some way to make you all the way human again, what would it be?"

Of course there is no answer to that.

"In the case of the boys-who-were-ducks," I continue, "it all hinged on bog cotton." I toss a bit of fluff in the air and watch it get carried away by the breeze. "In order to break the enchantment, the daughter had to pick enough bog cotton to weave each of her brothers a waistcoat, scarf, and cap. She managed her task, impossible as it was. She turned all her brothers back into humans, although one of them still had a wing because of an unfinished sleeve."

I turn to Spinning Girl. "It seems our task is as impossible as that, for somehow or other we have to find the goatman and get to the farm—and soon!"

Spinning Girl is not looking at me. Her eyes are cast down, and I follow her gaze. At our feet, in the white moss, is a drop of blood, red on the white reindeer moss. At first I think perhaps my nose has begun to bleed, but ahead of us there is another spot of blood. And ahead, another. And there, spattered on a flat stone. And there, a red stain on a patch of old snow, and on and on like this we go, following the drops of red on the moss and stones and snow.

And then—I almost let out a cry—a clump of alders, a patch of daisies, an opening in the woods. A place I recognize.

Here is a stone. Just a stone, but placed just so. It has no words carved on it, but even so, I recognize it. Under this very ground is where my mama lies.

I've never really understood why Mama wasn't buried in the churchyard, but Papa said here was best anyway. Here we could visit her every day, and she could keep an eye on our doings.

Below us is the log cottage where we lived then. The smell of it wafts up the hill to me. It seems as if I can smell the hay in the barn and the cows and the new spring grass all dotted over with violets, and in the house the cold fireplace and the musty trunk, empty now, of course. I can smell it all and more. I can smell all the way back to my childhood.

It even seems for a moment that *I can hear the scrape of chairs on the floor of the house, and the rustle of skirts. And women's voices, hushed and intent.*

Behind the voices, the distant lowing of cows, the cry of a rooster, a child's ceaseless wailing. And an old woman sitting at the hearth, heating something over the fire.

✖✦✦✦✖

I shake this strange memory away and tell Spinning Girl, "Stay here awhile." She slumps onto the grass gratefully.

Then it's only a short walk before I look down on Aunt and Uncle's farm. The buildings of the farm below make a kind of circle around a central yard, which I can't see from this angle but where I know there is a well, and worn paths from the house to the barn, from the house to the privy, from the house to the storehouse and the cow barn, the drying house, goat house, henhouse, woodshed, potato cellar, toolshed—all the outbuildings.

I might have been the mistress here one day myself if Papa had been born a few moments earlier. But Papa was not the eldest twin, and it's the eldest son who inherits the farm—that's the law. Still, Papa stayed on the farm as a cotter—an extra hand—until Mama died. Then the farm fell on hard times and couldn't support us all. And why was that? Not for lack of soil or livestock; it was Aunt, who squandered anything extra on fine things for her daughters. "Their dowries," she claimed, and filled their chests with linen tablecloths, pewter candlesticks, butter presses, ale bowls, lace curtains, and crisp, white aprons while our little family went hungry.

I creep down the hill and crouch behind a barrel in the shade of the cow barn, keeping my eyes peeled for Svaalberd. A lift of the lid and a dunk of a finger is all it takes to discover the barrel's contents: beer. There are two barrelsful, which is something to wonder over. Another thing to wonder over is where everyone is. The farm seems strangely quiet, but perhaps they are all out in the fields, engaged in some chore.

Shh! There goes the goatman, creeping from chicken house to hay shed. As soon as he's inside, I race across the yard and dart into the house.

No one is home, but what is this? The table is laid with a new lace tablecloth. On top of that sits the largest tub of sour-cream porridge I've ever seen. Surrounding it are

—platters heaped high with flatbread and rounds

of crisp *knäkkebrød*;

—thinly sliced cured ham, smoked mutton, and
   spiced sausages;
—an enormous plate of scrambled eggs flecked
   with bright specks of green chives;
—a vat of pea soup;
—tiny new carrots and peas, steamed and glossy
   with freshly churned butter;
—and cakes of all kinds: almond, marzipan, and
   one slathered with whipped cream and dotted
   all over with cherries and plums (now one
   plum less)

and everything as pretty as can be.

I can't stop staring at it all. But there's movement out
the window, and I duck down by the table. A glance tells me
that Svaalberd is hobbling across the farmyard. He stops and
swings his head from side to side, whether from puzzlement
or pain, I cannot say. While I wait for him to decide where he's
headed, I slice into the marzipan cake and take a piece. It is so
soft and sweet, something I have only heard of, never tasted,
and I wonder how this abundance has come to pass.

In the story of the girl and the bear, when the girl left the
bear's castle to go home to visit her family, she found them
living in splendor. They had everything they wished for: food
and fine things and so much joy that there was no end to it.

I stare again at the table laden with food. At the fresh

white tablecloth. The pretty lace curtains. The piece of cake in my hand. Is it enchanted, this cake? And all of this? Magic that will turn into vapor at any moment?

Just in case, I stuff the rest of the piece in my mouth.

With a start, I see that Svaalberd is stomping in my direction. I climb out the opposite window, alighting on the grass on the far side of the house.

Now, here's an odd thing: All of my cousins' everyday dresses are spread out in the grass as if the girls had been napping there and suddenly disappeared, leaving their dresses behind. Here their white stockings are lying like puddles of dirty snow. And here their everyday aprons. There's a sour taste in my mouth now, like you might get if the cake you just ate was baked from deviltry.

Then I notice the buckets and the soap and the cloths for drying, and realize they must have been washing here and left their clothes to dry in the sun. There is a lump of soap right there, probably the very soap I helped make out of ashes and tallow but never was allowed to use. Well. As I've now become a thief, I don't see the harm in taking one more thing, especially something I made myself. Into the sack it goes.

Peeking around the corner, I watch as Svaalberd exits the house and crosses the yard. That is when I notice something that explains everything: several long tables lined up end to end in the middle of the yard, all covered neatly in crisp white tablecloths, the edges fluttering in the breeze.

And then I know where everyone is.

Past the tables, down the hillside, winding along the road from the valley below, comes a moving river of dark colors and white splotches. The dark colors are men's jackets and women's skirts; the white splotches are the women's bright aprons and blouses. I can hear the fiddle now; its happy tones waft up the hill toward the farm.

Even from this distance, the glint and glimmer of the bridal crown makes me catch my breath. A bridal crown! Which of my cousins is the lucky bride? I wonder. I squint and pull at the corners of my eyes to see which girl it is, but all I can see is the glittering of the silver crown upon her head. However did Aunt pay for *that*? And how did she pay for the pounds of rice and raisins and sugar for the pudding and the barrels of beer? She would have had to sell something. But what did she have left to sell?

What looks like every living soul in the valley troops along behind the newly married couple up toward the farm, where they will have a feast of sausages, pea soup, and pudding, the beer from the barrels in the shade of the barn, and the cake with one slice missing.

The crunch of footfalls sends my heart catapulting into my throat. Svaalberd! Where is he now? I peek around the side of the house and see him crossing to the privy. Well, I know what to do about that!

The very moment he steps inside, I run across the yard, slam the door, and throw shut the iron latch—the latch that works only from the outside and that keeps the door from banging on windy days or lets others know the little house is unoccupied.

Just in time, too, because the procession is nearing the farm.

Then I race across the yard and fling myself under the table. In the meantime, old Goatbeard pounds with his fists, cursing a blue streak. But the fiddler plays, the women are "Don't you look fine?"-ing, the men "Oh is that so?"-ing. Children chase each other in play, shrieking with delight. Not a soul hears poor old Svaalberd banging on the outhouse door.

By lifting one corner of the tablecloth, I have quite a good view of the proceedings: There is Aunt, her face flushed with triumph as she nods smugly to the women, smiles haughtily at the men, and laughs indulgently at the children, who are wiping their sweaty faces on the table linens. And there are my cousins, trying to out-pretty each other in front of the boys. Meanwhile Greta runs back and forth, carrying trays and plates and bowls from the house to the tables.

Aunt invites the guests to the table and then turns to the parson. "Will you lead us in the table prayer, Reverend?" she asks ever so sweetly.

Everyone bows their heads in preparation for prayer. Even Svaalberd is quiet. Perhaps he's praying someone will let him out.

I suppose I should be praying, too, and praying for all I'm worth, but I'm watching for Greta. And here she comes out of the house carrying the marzipan cake—Aunt's eyes flash toward the missing slice, then narrow to slits as she stares at Greta.

The parson begins his prayer: "Gracious God in heaven."

"The devil in blackest hell!" a voice calls from the outhouse.

Heads remain bowed, although eyes flicker upward. Still, the parson goes on. "We humbly beseech you—"

"By Lucifer, open this cursed door!" Svaalberd shouts.

"—to bless these thy gifts—" continues the parson.

"Curse you to all eight hells!" Svaalberd hollers and, with a crash and a clatter, bursts open the door. Out he flies, head-first like a billy goat, and runs down the little slope and comes charging, arms spinning, into the crowd.

Uncle steps aside to avoid being knocked down, and the wild-eyed goatman flies past him, then staggers about in the middle of the farmyard, his face purple with rage. He curses, shakes his shaggy head, and waves his bloody, bandaged hand.

"You wretched lot who locked me in the privy should be ashamed!" he cries.

The wedding guests stand as if turned to stone.

"Here I have come now to seek restitution. That girl you

sold me turned out to be a worthless wench who never did a decent day's work." (That is a lie.) "She stole my money." (That is true.) "And she—"

Aunt interrupts him. "You must have done something to deserve it, you old goat," she says.

"What did I do to deserve *this*?" he screams, flinging off his bandages and waving his bloody stumps at the crowd. Blood spatters on white blouses and aprons. Women shriek; men back away; children cower.

Only Aunt stands her ground. "Now, Svaalberd," she says, "you'd best go home and take care of that wound. You can see we've got a festive occasion—"

"Which you've spent plenty on, by the look of it; I can see that, all right!" he shouts. "Festivity or no, I need a new girl. I'll take"—he points one of his mutilated fingers at the bride, who clings, trembling, to her new husband, also trembling—"that one."

"She's only just married," Aunt says.

"Then this one," Svaalberd says, seizing Katinka's long braid.

"No!" Aunt cries, rushing to her. "She'll be married herself soon."

Meanwhile, I'm scrambling along under the long table as fast as I can go, my eyes on the far end, at Greta's little white stockings surrounded by grown-up legs. In the meantime, I can hear Svaalberd making his way along the line of girls toward Greta.

Aunt has an excuse for each one:

"She's half-deaf."

"This one'll never give you a day's work."

"That one's lame."

"I need a girl to replace the one who's run away!" Svaalberd shouts. "I need a girl!"

"You can have the youngest," Aunt says. "You can have Greta."

Which one of us, I wonder, wriggling along—all bruised knees and pounding heart—which one of us, me or the goat-man, will reach her first?

"Where is she, then?" Svaalberd booms.

I imagine everyone's head swiveling, looking around for tiny Greta, so easily swallowed up in a sea of adults. So much smaller than you'd think for a girl of eight.

"Why"—it's Aunt's voice again—"she was there just a moment ago."

I see Aunt's hand reaching for the edge of the tablecloth.

"Again you try to cheat me!" Svaalberd roars.

The tablecloth is thrown back, and while Greta and I cling to each other, we catch glimpses of Svaalberd choking Aunt, then Uncle leaping onto the goatman's back. The goatman twists and turns and finally manages to fling Uncle into the watering trough.

Some men rush to help Uncle, others try to subdue Svaalberd, while still others have cracked the beer barrels and are quaffing their thirst while taking bets on the outcome.

Chairs are overturned, the porridge pot upended. Chickens come scuttling to peck at the crusts and crumbles that spill from the table. Even a goat prances over, climbs a chair, and is now on the table munching something. The almond cake, most like.

In the meantime, Greta and I make our long way under the tables to the end closest to the trees.

"Little sister," I say to her. "We are going to America."

She nods yes. *Yes!* she nods.

"Do you need to get anything before we leave?" I whisper.

She shakes her head no. It's a stab to my heart that in the midst of all this plenty, she has nothing to fetch.

"Well," I whisper, "we're not leaving without some of this feast!"

Out we jump and join the chickens, who are grabbing cardamom buns, sliced ham, and sausages. Into the sack it all goes, and Greta and I head for the trees.

The beer has done its work, for men are throwing punches at each other, settling old scores. The bridegroom has joined the beer drinkers, and the bride is slumped in a chair, weeping. This is the last thing I see as Greta and I, our sack stuffed with food and treasure, dash into the woods on the far side of the farm. And the last thing I hear ringing in my ears is my Aunt's shrill voice yelling, "There they are! The two girls! There they go!"

II

Flight

The Golden Wreath

H ow fine would it be to have the winds carry you to the far corners of the earth, or anywhere you want to go, like they did for the girl in the story? Or even to run, as you might imagine you would escape, through the cow pasture, then through the aspen grove, leaves flickering above you, and finally out into the sunny meadow, startling up swallows that swoop and wheel.

If you think that's how it goes, then you have forgotten about Spinning Girl, whom we have retrieved from the cotter's hut and now coax and cajole along as best we can.

Instead of running, we stumble, while I cast glances over my shoulder, expecting the entire wedding party to catch up to us at any moment. But we are small girls, and we find little grottoes and hiding places along the way. When the pursuers get too close, we duck within a cluster of big boulders.

Tucked in the cool shadows, we barely breathe. I clamp my hand over Spinning Girl's keys to keep them still, while Greta holds a finger to her lips.

There are shouts and the pounding of feet, which run past

us and away. Finally, after the voices fade, we three girls creep out from our hiding spot and start off again, moving west.

✤✤✤✤✤

I n a meadow near a small lake, we plop ourselves down on the heather. The sun is just a red-gold globe hovering low in the sky, so it must be very late. This time of year, the sun will barely sink below the horizon before it pops back up again.

Out of the sack comes the tablecloth. The cloth is spread with the spoils of the wedding feast, and oh! we're as hungry as bears. While we stuff ourselves with sausages and cake, I explain to Greta what I know about Spinning Girl, and I tell her how things went at the goatman's farm. Not all of it, but some.

Meanwhile, Spinning Girl weaves wreaths of primroses and bluebells. She's handy with her fingers, that one. When she's finished, she places a wreath on each of our heads.

"What I have been wondering over," Greta says, "is how we are going to get to America."

"Oh, as to that," I tell her, "I have it all thought out." I don't, of course, but there's no need to tell Greta that. "All we need," I continue, "is a golden apple, a golden spinning wheel, and a golden carding comb, like the girl in the story had."

"We have lots of golden things," Greta says, gesturing to the meadow around us. "Look!"

In the yellow twilight, every tassel, frond, pine needle,

speck of moss, and shred of heather is tipped with silver or threaded with gold. The lake beyond gleams like a plate of hammered copper. And just over the rise beyond the lake, the sun glows—"like Soria Moria Castle," I say. "And that's the direction we have to go to get to America."

"Soria Moria," she repeats, and peers off that way as if she might catch a glimpse of it. Then she exclaims, "But look! Look at my emerald bracelet!" She holds up her arm to show me an iridescent green beetle that clings to her wrist.

"And the ruby earrings dangling from the bushes!" I say.

"And the jeweled necklaces strung between the branches!" she adds.

"And your golden curls, Greta."

"What about your hair, Astri? What color do you think it is?"

I put my hand to my hair, which feels like sticky cobwebs. "What color is it now?" I ask.

"It's kind of . . . gray."

"Gray! Like an old lady's?"

"No, gray like dusty old straw at the end of winter," Greta says. "But only because it's so dirty."

"The goatman never let me wash it—not once!" I complain. "He was afraid I would fall ill from having wet hair. And you know he couldn't afford to let me have a day off work just for being ill!"

"And Aunt never let you wash your hair, either."

"I wonder why."

"I think she didn't want you catching the eye of any young man who might come courting our cousins," Greta muses. She curls up and pulls a corner of the tablecloth over herself.

"Do you really think so?" I take the wreath from my head and hold it up to the last glimmer of the dying sun. For a moment it had been as golden as the wreath the girl in the story had wanted so badly. But now the sun is gone and the color fading from the meadow.

What have I done? I wonder. What kind of trouble have I gotten us into? And what will become of us?

The Birch Tree

n the story of the girl and the bear, when the girl woke after she'd dropped the tallow on the shirt of the handsome prince, she found herself on a little green field in the middle of a gloomy, thick forest, and by her side lay the same bundle with her old rags that she had brought from home.

And so it is for me, for when I wake, I am lying on a little grassy patch in the midst of a gloomy forest. Gone is the golden meadow and the lake made of hammered copper and the red-gold sun. The rubies, emeralds, and jeweled necklaces of the night before have been replaced by dusty raspberries, buzzing dragonflies, and cobwebs strung from branch to branch. And there, in the heather, are Spinning Girl and Greta, still asleep.

Mist rises from the lake like the smoke from old men's pipes. I rise quietly, pick up the gunnysack, and walk down to the water's edge. Peering into the black water, I see a girl's reflection, both familiar and unfamiliar. For a moment I think I am seeing the face of Spinning Girl. I look up, expecting to see her, but she is not there. It is just a ripple in the water that distorted the reflection, which is mine: dark eyes set in pale cheeks, dust-colored hair, upon which rests the wreath, now limp and colorless. This I set aside.

Off comes my dress, and into my hand goes the lump of soap. Then into the icy water I wade, in just my muslin under-shift. I unwind my braids, dip my head into the water, and lather my hair. A cloud of grease, grime, and soot settles on the surface, which I push away with my hands, then rinse my hair in the clear water.

I think of the bewitched princess who, in order to have her troll-hide removed, was scrubbed in whey, then rubbed in sour milk.

Like her, I am scrubbed clean, but instead of sweet and pretty, I feel my skin tightening in the cold water, becoming taut and tough as a gristly old troll-hide. The water pricks all over like needles, and I set my mind to *never mind*: Never mind about the cold water, and never mind about the hardships to come.

For a moment, everything is strangely still and silent. Even the dragonflies have alighted on something. All I hear is the water dripping from my hair into the lake. *Tap tap tap.*

Then the screech of a raven draws my eye to the shore, where something rises, peering, above the bushes.

I squint.

A bear? Snout in the air, sniffing? Maybe it is a bear like in the story. Well, not exactly, because this bear isn't white. Natu-rally, I wouldn't get a *white* bear for my story, but a dirty, dingy, sooty-looking one with a hump. *That* is not a bear!

There, through the mist, a dark figure, now with *two* humps on his back, one that wiggles and thrashes! It's the goatman, all right, and the second hump is my sister thrown over his shoulder.

In a thrice, I am on the shore. "Put her down," I yell at him, snatching up the gunnysack, "or I drop the sack in the lake!" I twist the top of the sack to make a knot, then swing the sack in bigger and bigger arcs, and holler, "I'll toss it in if you don't put her down!"

The goatman moves to the lakeshore and dangles Greta over the water. "Throw the sack over to me now, or I'll throw the *girl* in the pond," he hollers back. He lets go of one of her arms, and Greta gives a little involuntary shriek.

"You throw her in and I'll throw the sack in, and we'll see which one sinks faster," I say to him. I've got him there.

Svaalberd sets Greta down but keeps hold of her arm, even though she tugs and squirms.

"Give me the sack and I'll let the girl go," he says.

"Let go of the girl and I'll give you the sack," I tell him.

Now we're as stuck as two moose with their antlers locked. And how to untangle them?

He's calculating. His face twitches with the effort. He knows he's fast and strong. He might, he thinks, be able to release Greta, then grab the sack, and me, and Greta again, all three, before we can get away.

And I am thinking the same thing. That is, I know *I* could elude him, but I don't know if Greta and Spinning Girl can. And speaking of Spinning Girl, where is she?

Then suddenly, she is there, jangling the ring of keys. The goatman jerks with surprise and lurches toward her. Greta twists free. He lunges back to grab at her, but she darts away. The two girls skitter about like chickens in a farmyard, and the goatman whirls and twists, trying to catch first one, then the other, as if trying to grab one for the stew pot. Meantime, my mind whirls and twists and lunges and grasps at anything, any idea, any solution, but—nothing.

There's a strange noise—a cough, maybe, or a squeal and a snort. It's Spinning Girl. She's got her head thrown back, and sound comes from her mouth! She's laughing! She thinks this is a game—like the one my cousins used to play, where one person was "it" and had to try to tag the others. And then I realize: This is probably the only time in her whole life she's ever played a game.

Spinning Girl's laughter makes me want to laugh; it makes me want to stop everything and hug her. And for a moment it takes away my dizzying fear, just long enough to think. To think of what to do.

I rush toward the goatman and he twists and starts, then plunges after me. I slide my arm through the knot in the sack, grasp hold of one of the smooth-skinned birch trees, and up I go like a bear cub: feet, knees, elbows, hands, in a way I didn't even know I knew.

And there he is below, standing like a bear with his claws raking the tree trunk, head tipped back, glaring up at me. Greta and Spinning Girl stare, too, with their mouths agape, as if I am on fire. I can't ask why they're staring so hard—there's no time for that.

I just shout, "Run, little sister! Run, Spinning Girl! Run to Soria Moria."

⁂

Sometimes goats get up in trees, eating the leaves, when there's nothing else to eat. How they get there you never know; you just see them standing on branches, munching away. So I'm not surprised to see old Goatbeard himself climbing the tree after me.

That's fine. The longer I can distract him, the farther away the girls can get. I just keep shimmying up the tree: hands, elbows, knees, and feet. Here, in the crotch of the tree, I set the sack, untie the knot, and reach inside.

"Is this what you want, old man?" I call down to him, dropping a handful of coins. The first one *ping*s against his upturned forehead while others shower around him.

He roars, snatching at the air as the coins whistle by his ears.

I reach into the sack again, find Mama's brooch, and pin it

onto my shift. And up the tree I go. And up he comes after me.

Up I go, and up he comes. Soon, though, even my slight weight is too much, and the tree begins to bend, slowly bowing its crown toward earth. Holding on to the trunk, I let my legs dangle, suspended between earth and sky, willing the tree to bend a little more, a little more. The ground rushes up. I wait . . . wait . . . then fling myself off the tree, arms wheeling, legs kicking. Deprived of my weight, the tree springs back, with the goatman still clinging to the trunk.

Leaves flutter down. Among them, I see the Black Book, the wedding crumbs, the old potatoes, and many, many coins, tumbling and flipping in the air, catching the sunlight that breaks through the mist.

As for me, I am a bird, a cloud, a falling star. As I hurtle through the sky, all that *was* burns up behind me in a hot white tail, and all that *will be* rushes toward me, cool and green. Good-bye, I say, to what was. Good-bye to the golden meadow and the lake of hammered copper. Good-bye to the emerald bracelets, the ruby earrings, and the jeweled necklaces strung between the branches.

As the goatman scrambles down the tree and rushes about plucking up coin after scattered coin, I say good-bye to the treasure.

Then I snatch up my dress and shoes and run up and over the hill, into the sun, west to Soria Moria.

The Magic Ball of Yarn

"**A** stri," Greta says, as we three girls struggle up the mountainside, "isn't America terribly far away? How are we ever going to get all the way there?"

"Do you know the story of the girl and the white bear?" I ask. "How, on her journey to find the bear she had lost, the girl was given things? A magic tablecloth. A pair of scissors that snipped and played so that pieces of silk and strips of velvet flew about her if she but clipped in the air."

"In the story of the girl and the bear, it was the girl following the bear, not the other way around," Greta says, glancing over her shoulder.

I cast a glance behind me and see a speck moving up the mountain behind us. "Can you tell who that is?" I ask Greta.

"It's him," she says.

"All we need," I tell her, "is a magic ball of yarn that, when you toss it in front of you, leads you where you want to go. Then we'll be fine."

We have come upon a *seter* hut, so I say, "And perhaps here is where we'll get that yarn."

Out comes the milkmaid, shoving up her sleeves. *"Hie!"*

she says when she sees us. "Here are some tired lasses! Where are you bound, and from whence do you come?"

I tell her where we're from, and that we're going to America.

"America! Nay!" she says, pulling her head back.

"Aye, that's where we're bound," I repeat.

"Why, that's very far away."

"That it is," I agree.

"And costs ever so dearly! Why, folks sell their farms and all their stock and equipment to get enough money for a venture like that," she says, eyeing our ragged clothes.

"I suppose that's so," I tell her. "Nonetheless, that's where we're bound."

"But say," she says, "you must be frightfully hungry! Wouldn't you like something to eat?"

The girls look at me hopefully. There wasn't any breakfast, nor, until now, any prospect of one. I glance over my shoulder. The speck is still but a speck.

"I suppose you haven't got a magic ball of yarn?" I ask. "That when you toss it in front of you leads you where you want to go?"

The milkmaid laughs and says no, she hasn't anything like that. "But wait right here," she says. Into the hut she goes, and out she comes again carrying a bowl sloshing with milk.

"Drink that," she says, "before you perish from thirst. And when you're finished, I'll give you this." She pulls a hairbrush from her pocket.

"A hairbrush?" I ask, while Greta and Spinning Girl take turns slurping milk.

"For your hair! Once you get the tangles out, it will be devilish pretty to look at."

"Pretty?" I touch my hair. I had forgotten that I'd washed it; its silky softness surprises me.

"Why," Greta says, handing me the bowl, "it's so pretty, it looks like gold might fall out of it every time you brush it."

"Gold falling from my hair! I've never heard the like of that!" I say, and swallow down the last of the milk.

"There are more things in heaven and earth than can be dreamed," the dairymaid says. "An Englishman told me so."

"In spite of that," I say, "it seems true enough."

The dairymaid takes the bowl, now empty, and hands me the hairbrush. Then she tells us that to get to America, we'll have to go to the fjord that leads to the sea. "You'll have to go down—down to the valley, that way." She points. "And follow the trail that leads along the river. There are farms down there and a village. And farther along, the fjord."

I thank her kindly, and as we are starting our way down the hill, she calls to us in a cheery voice, "Take care! I've heard that sometimes the emigrants never make it to America, but are sent to Turkey and sold as slaves!"

Greta stares at me, her eyes wide.

"Even in America, I've heard tell," the milkmaid says, her voice low and serious, "they keep slaves."

I turn slowly back to face her. "Nay!" I say. "That can't be true."

"'Tis ," she says darkly.

The three of us turn and walk away in silence, pondering this.

"She's but a simple dairymaid," I say, finally. "Even so, she's been helpful enough, for she's told us where we need to go. And that is just about as good as a magic ball of yarn."

The Bridge

For a long time, every time I cast a glance over my shoulder, I can see the dark, wobbly splotch that is Svaalberd following us. But now, coming down into the trees, I can't see much. It's hard to know if he's near or far, here or there, even if he's ahead or behind.

"What we could really use now is a pair of seven-league boots," I tell the girls.

"You mean the kind of boots that take you fifteen miles every time you take a step?" Greta says. "Do you think there really are such things?"

"There are more things in heaven and earth than can be dreamed," I tell her. "As the dairymaids say."

We're following a path along the river. Down and down we go, into a gloomy gorge. Greta walks hand in hand with Spinning Girl, while I take up the rear.

Eventually, we come to a bridge. We would hurry right across, but a noise stops us.

"You don't suppose there's a troll living under that bridge, do you?" Greta says. We listen for a moment to what sounds like the rumbling of an enormous stomach and the smacking of giant lips.

"No," I tell her, not sure at all. "That's just the river growling and smacking. Just in case, here's what we'll do. You take Spinning Girl across and tell the troll not to waste his time on such little morsels as you. Tell him to wait for your sister, who is much bigger and tastier and who is coming along right behind you."

"No!" Greta says. "For then he'll eat you!"

"Oh, no," I tell her, "for I know a trick or two myself."

Holding Spinning Girl's hand, Greta steps out onto the bridge. "Trip trop, trip trop," she says, "here we come, the tiniest girls you ever did see. But wait a moment and my sister will come by, and she's much bigger and tastier than both of us put together." The two girls step off the bridge on the far side of the river.

Now it's my turn. The growling of the river has grown louder and hungrier sounding. "Troll," I announce, "if troll you are, I want to point out that I am not a goat, just a goat girl. Hardly a mouthful. What you must do is wait a bit for the goatman who will surely be coming along soon enough. He's much bigger and tastier than I and has a hump on his back that would carve up into a nice roast for Sunday dinner, if you don't mind my mentioning Sunday."

"Does he now?" peals a voice like a bell. It's so clear and

real I feel the fine hairs on the back of my neck stand up. Then I hear the sound of splashing, like someone or something wading about in the water under the bridge.

"Indeed, I think that's what I'll do—eat you up!" says the voice. "Yum! Yum! Yum!"

"That's not what you're supposed to say," I squeak.

"'Tisn't?" comes the voice.

"No," say I. "You're supposed to say, 'Very well, then, be off with you.'"

"Maybe I would have said *that* if *you* had said you were going up the hill to get fat, but you didn't. Also, you are not going up the hill but down it."

I watch as the top of a head appears, then a pair of shoulders, then the whole of a person. It's a boy carrying a fishing pole and a stringer of fish. And laughing!

"Well, you're little, that's certain," says he, "but if you're a goat girl, then where are your goats?"

"I've left them at the farm of the man who owns them," I say.

"Is that the man with the hump?"

"That's the one. He hasn't come by this way, I suppose?"

"Nay," says the boy. "But let's ask my ma, for not much gets past her!"

We follow the boy along the well-worn trail, as sheep run ahead of us, their bells clanging in the rosy twilight. After a bit, we come into a farmyard where the lad's ma is out pitching scraps to a litter of piglets. The boy introduces us as Little Girl, Littler Girl, and Littlest Girl, and his ma trundles off to the house with the stringer of fish.

Later, as we scrape our bread around on the plates, sopping up every bit of juice, the farmwife asks, "How do such wee lasses come here all by themselves, I wonder?" She chucks Greta on the chin.

"Well, our ma died," I explain, "and so my sister and I had to go live with our mean aunt."

"That was poor luck," says she.

"Not such terrible luck, for our pa went to America to get rich so he could send money for us to join him," I tell them.

"Oh, that is fine luck, then!" says the boy.

"But in the meantime, my mean aunt sold me to an even meaner master," I say.

"Oh, that was terrible bad luck!" says the farmwife.

"Not *so* terrible, for the mean old man had a troll treasure laid up in his house," I tell her.

"Treasure!" the boy exclaims. "Is that so, then?"

"It's so, indeed, for I laid hands on it and ran away and fetched my sister, and now we're setting off for America to find our papa."

"That's fine luck, then!" the boy chimes in.

"Not such good luck, after all," I say, "for the old man caught up with us and got the treasure back!"

At this, the farmwife and her son exhale sighs of deepest disappointment, while I wonder where he's gotten to, old Mr. Svaalberd.

The farmwife takes away our plates. "You lasses sleep here," she says, "as it is getting late. My hens are laying, so there'll be fresh eggs for breakfast, so don't be in too much of a hurry to rush off, neither. We won't send you away with empty stomachs!"

She then clamps eyes on Spinning Girl, who's fallen asleep in a chair. "That one looks plumb worn out, poor thing," she says, then whispers, "Is there something a wee bit wrong with her?"

I shrug. "She doesn't say much, so it's hard to know if anything is wrong with her or not," I say. "When it comes to spinning, there's not her like to be found."

"Is that so?" the woman says, casting a more respectful eye on the girl. "Well, they're for bed, these two." To me she says, "You, stay here."

While the farmwife makes beds of sheepskins on the floor, I glance out the window, wondering if Svaalberd is outside circling the farmhouse at this very moment.

Once the girls are tucked in under their woolly blankets,

the woman turns to me. "First of all," she says, "I'm going to brush your hair, which sorely needs it. I don't suppose you have a brush, for you seem to have nothing at all."

"Why, there you are wrong," I proclaim, producing the hairbrush the dairymaid gave me.

"You're full of surprises, you are," she says as she puts the brush to my scalp. Right away it gets hung up in the tangles. These she picks apart with her fingers, as if pulling dirt from wool. "So you've caught America fever like so many others!" she says, sighing. "Just like the three billy goats, folks are—the grass always looks tastier somewhere else!" She clucks her tongue and tugs and pulls at my hair until my scalp aches. "But what I wonder is, where are all the things you need for such a journey as that?" she says. "It seems you're going off to America without anything, when most others bring their whole lot with them, plus food for twelve weeks of sailing: bread and whey cheese and dried meat and mutton and butter and sour milk and potatoes and all."

She ticks off a list of things we should take, and the list is so long that the brush begins to move smoothly through my tresses. I wonder when the coins will start falling from my hair, but they never do. There's just an ache that travels from my scalp down to where I guess my heart is. Is this what it's like to have a mother? I wonder. Did I wriggle and squirm long ago when Mama brushed my hair? I don't remember. Now I am as still as a church mouse, feeling these brush strokes in my heart.

"You could stay here with me, you girls," the farmwife says softly. "It's a mite lonely now, without my husband, and I've always wanted a daughter." She sighs, and I wonder: What if we stayed here, the three of us, and this kind woman could be our mother? Spinning Girl would spin the wool of their sheep, and Greta would make everyone happy, as she always does, and I . . . Well, I don't seem to be good at anything at all, unless it's making trouble.

Seven-League Boots

The first thing I see when I open my eyes is Spinning Girl. She's been up all night spinning straw into gold, by the looks of it. Beautiful yarn she's made—as if shot through with golden threads! The farmwife is turning it over in her hands, admiring it.

"'Tis fine, indeed!" the woman coos.

"'Twould be hard to find its like," I tell Spinning Girl, and she gives me a skein of it. Looking closer, I can see what those shining threads really are—not gold at all, but strands of hair. *My* hair!

My hand goes to my head, and I feel the smooth softness of brushed hair. Then I remember that the farmwife brushed it the night before when she told me about all the things we needed for a trip to America. These things crowd my mind: food and cooking pots and bedding and money to pay for our passage and such as that. And how are we going to get all that, now that we haven't got the treasure? Perhaps we *should* stay here with the farmwife and her son. One glance at Spinning Girl's glowing face, and I can guess that she'd be happy here.

But, oh! Have we come only this far to give up already? What about America? What about Papa?

If we could get that treasure back, we'd be able to buy our passage and our food and all the things we need for the journey to America. But I can't imagine that we have time to go looking all over the place for the goatman—maybe all the way back to the goat farm—before the ship sails! Especially, I think, glancing at Spinning Girl, considering how slowly we move. The only way to get the treasure back is with a pair of seven-league boots.

As I puzzle over this, I become aware of the sounds of a farm at full daylight: a rooster crowing, the baaing of sheep, the whinny of horses. And that gives me an idea.

"Well," says the farmwife, "I've promised you eggs, haven't I?" And off she trundles across the farmyard with a basket over her arm.

As soon as she's gone, here comes the lad. "Off to America, then?" says he.

"Aye, that we are," I tell him, glancing around the room for my shoes.

"What about your cook pots and your food? You have to bring food for the voyage, you know. Bread and cheese and meat and herring—everything! It seems you haven't got a thing."

"Why, as to that, I have it all thought out. All we really need right now is a pair of seven-league boots," I tell him, snagging one of my shoes from under the table. "You haven't a pair of those, have you?"

He laughs and says no, he hasn't.

"That's too bad," I say, "because if I had a pair of seven-league boots, I could catch up with the old man and get the treasure back, I shouldn't wonder. Then I'd have so much gold I wouldn't know what to do with it all."

"Is that so?" the boy says. "You wouldn't know what to do with it?"

"I wouldn't be able to carry it, even," I say, hopping on one foot while sliding my shoe on the other. "But since I don't have any of those boots, I don't suppose there's any way to catch up with him. Maybe if I had a horse. Maybe just. Oh, but I haven't got a horse, have I? What a foolish thing to think about."

"*We* have horses!" cries the boy.

"Have you?" I respond, though I can see them well enough out the window, flicking flies off their flanks with their long, glossy tails.

"I'll tell you what," says the boy. He glances out the door as his mother disappears into the henhouse. "You can ride our Dapple to the man's house, get the treasure, bring it back here, pick up the two girls, and off you go. Whatever portion of the treasure you don't want to carry, you can leave with me for safekeeping."

"Hmm," I say. "Well, it's not exactly a pair of seven-league boots, is it? But it's better than nothing. Still, what would your ma say about you lending out her horse like that?"

"She won't even notice," says the lad. "'Tis I who tends to the horses. Just make sure you bring him back straightaway, you know, once you've got the treasure."

"That's a fine offer, indeed," I say, nabbing my other shoe from behind a chair, "but I don't know . . . I'm terribly fearful of horses."

"I'm not!" Greta pipes up, as I knew she would.

"Aye, that's so," I agree, "but you're far too small to carry the treasure by yourself."

"You shall come with me, then!" she sings and claps her hands. "And that will be jolly!"

I turn to look at the boy, but he's already walking to the pasture gate to fetch the horse.

In the meantime, I turn to Spinning Girl. "We're off on an errand," I tell her.

She reaches for a length of yarn that is looped around her neck. At the end of the loop, I see now, dangles a key, shiny and pretty as a bit of jewelry. She takes it from her neck and hangs it around mine, where I feel its coolness against my skin.

A key! I've never had a key to anything. Never had anything worth locking up, in fact. Except Mama's brooch, of course.

Well. Here comes the boy returning with the horse, all saddled and bridled and ready to go.

Quickly, without letting myself think about it, I unpin Mama's brooch from my dress and pin it on Spinning Girl's. By the look on her face, I'll wager she's never been given anything like it. Or any gift at all, most like. Still, somehow, I feel that it's I who have been given the greater gift.

The Seven-Headed Troll

A horse is a far better thing to have than a pair of seven-league boots, any day," I tell Greta. I am pleased with Dapple, who is healthy and not old either, and with the well-tooled saddle and the nice bridle with silver buckles. And with just me and Greta on his back, it's a comfortable ride.

Clip clop, go Dapple's hooves over the bridge, along the rushing river, back into the gloomy gorge.

"Oh, it's lovely to ride a horse instead of walking, and now we can get the treasure, and then we shall be rich as kings!" Greta says. "But, sister, I have been thinking. Wouldn't it be stealing, to take that treasure from Mr. Svaalberd?"

"No, it wouldn't, because old Svaalberd stole it from the trolls. That's nearly the only way you can get troll gold these days, and it isn't stealing to take something that's stolen already, is it?"

It has started to rain, and perhaps the ticking of the leaves or the *tap tap tap* of rain on the branches makes Dapple nervous, for he seems skittish, throwing his head back at the trembling of a leaf. He snorts, his breath a white cloud in the cool, damp air.

"I think something is moving in the trees," Greta whispers.

"That's just the bending of the boughs in the wind," I tell her. "Or the fluttering of birds."

The key that hangs from my neck taps against my chest, and I lift it up and look at it. What is it for, this key? Not to any of the outbuildings. Not to Svaalberd's precious chest. So small, it is. What, then?

"Sister," Greta says, after a while, "do you ever think that maybe Papa just hasn't been able to earn enough money to send for us yet? Maybe we should go back and wait a bit longer."

"We can't go back," I tell her, "either to the goat farm or to Aunt and Uncle's. So, then, where would we go?" I don't tell her of the farmwife's invitation.

"Astri," she says, "do you ever think Papa might be dead?"

"No!" I tell her. "I would know if he were dead."

"How?" Greta asks. "How would you know?"

I pull back on the reins, and Dapple stops. We've moved away from the rushing river and now follow a placid stream. Behind the murmur of the brook and the pattering of rain, I can hear the general hum of the world. I can feel it. And there is not an essential part of it missing, so Papa must be alive. But I don't know how to explain this to Greta, so I urge Dapple on while I tell Greta a story.

"One time, when I was little, younger even than you are now, Papa took me with him into the forest where he went to cut wood for charcoal. He set me in a little spot where the sun came down through the pine boughs and made a flickering patch of light.

"Suddenly, a dark shadow passed over me. I tipped my head back, like this, and what was standing over me but the most horrifying, most terrible, ugliest old *troll* you ever did see!"

"A troll!" Greta cries. *"Nie!"*

"Aye, a troll. The likes of which you wouldn't ever want to meet. And he picked me up, tucked me under his arm, and carried me off."

"Did you scream?"

"I screamed so loud there are valleys where you can hear me screaming still."

"What happened then?"

"He carried me off to his castle, where he made me sit all the day long and scratch his many heads." As I say this, it seems to me that I can even remember the smell of him, sour as a dozen old billy goats.

"How many heads did he have?"

"Oh, six or seven, I'd say."

"What happened?"

"Papa came to rescue me, of course."

"No!" Greta cries. "But how could he fight a troll?"

"That's just what I said! 'You'd better go home,' I said, 'for there's a troll here, and he will gobble you alive!' But Papa, he said he would stay and fight.

"'If that's to be the case,' I said, 'you had better use the troll's sword that's hanging over there on the wall.' Papa went to lift it, but he couldn't—it was far too heavy for any mortal to heft. So I told him that he'd better take a long pull from the troll's flask, for that was what the troll did every time he went to use the sword.'"

Dapple's ears twitch and turn. Are those footsteps I hear? It could just be the steady *tick tick tick* of rain on the leaves or the hammering of a woodpecker, some ways distant. Or maybe it's the beating of my heart against the key Spinning Girl gave me.

"What happened next, Astri?" Greta asks.

"Oh, well," I go on, "Papa took a long drink from the troll's flask, and in the twinkling of an eye, he could brandish the sword like nothing. And what should happen then but up came the troll, puffing and blowing.

"'*Hutetu*,' said the troll. 'What a stink there is of Christian blood!'

"'Don't you worry,' Papa said, 'you won't be bothered by that smell for long!' And with that, he hewed off all seven of the troll's heads, and the troll fell dead.'"

As I say this, it's as if I remember the dim halls of that

castle, the torches glimmering and the smudgelike shadows on the walls, the look of that great, gleaming sword and the leather drinking flask, and the rancid, old-man smell of the troll and his many greasy heads.

Dapple turns his head; his nostrils tremble. Perhaps he smells it, too, or maybe we are smelling last year's moldy leaves, the scent of them rising with each stamp of his hooves.

Greta clings to me, and all three of us fall silent as we ride through the tall trees, their trunks slick from the rain. It comes to me, steady and sure as the rain, that Svaalberd is here some-where, in this forest, watching us.

A nd then, there, lying in the middle of the path in front of us is a dirty-looking lump of something.

I pull back on the reins, and Dapple comes to a stop.

"It's a sack!" Greta cries. "Your gunnysack, isn't it? I'll go see!" She begins to slide off the horse's back, but I throw an arm behind me to stop her.

"Wait," I tell her.

Dapple throws back his head, nickers, stamps at the ground.

Where is Svaalberd? I wonder as I peer into the forest. All I see among the trees is an old stump weathered into a pale gray, a lump of dirty snow, a boulder. And no sign of the goatman.

Dapple is quiet now, and the only sound is the rain on the leaves.

I reach up and break two twigs off a rowan tree, one for me and one for Greta. "Put that sprig in your dress," I tell her, and slip a twig into the bodice of my own. "For protection."

We dismount and, with me holding the reins in one hand and Greta's hand in the other, creep slowly toward the sack.

The Spot of Tallow

It seems like an eternity, these steps to the gunnysack. My ears are pricked for any sound, any movement. But the sack is there—just lying there—and no sign of the goatman. I let go of Greta's hand to reach for it and she whispers, "That stump!" My skin prickles.

"That stump," she says, pointing to the side of the path, "has *eyes*!"

There, weathered as an old stump, craggy as stone, and sad as a lump of muddy snow, is the goatman. He stares up at us with a strange, twisted grin on his face, sitting propped up against a tree as if dead. But not dead, for his eyes move in their sockets, following us.

"Something is wrong with him," Greta whispers.

Sound comes from his throat, but no words from his crooked, frozen mouth.

Greta has let go of my arm and moves toward him.

"Get back!" I cry. "Don't touch him!"

But already her hand rests on his forehead, which sets him quaking all over like a wet dog shaking himself dry.

"Let's get away from here!" I say.

"We can't leave him like this!" Greta kneels down next to him.

"Little sister, move away," I plead. "It might be that the devil got hold of him."

"He's ill, is what," she says. "And look at his hand!"

The flesh around the wounded fingers is bluish gray, and the rest of his hand an angry red, puffed up to half again its normal size.

"That's a hideous sight," I tell her, "and how you can keep looking at it, I don't know." I turn my head away. Still, out of the corner of my eye, I see him watching me.

His eyes are the only part of his face that seem able to move, and he swivels them in my direction. They drift over my hair and face, then clasp on the key around my neck as if it might cure him.

I tuck the key into the bodice of my dress and button my sweater over it.

"Do you think we should take him to the village?" Greta says. "Maybe there would be someone who could help him."

"We'd have to get him on the horse, I suppose," I say. Dapple's nostrils widen; his eyes roll back, and he pulls against his reins as if he understands. "I doubt either one of them could withstand it."

"Maybe his fits will pass, and then we can decide what to do," Greta says. "Or someone will come by."

So here we sit. Greta dips a torn corner of the tablecloth into the stream and dabs it at Svaalberd's fevered face when he can tolerate it. I think about how the girl in the story sat by her bear-turned-prince's bed, unable to wake him. Night after night she sat there, weeping, while he slept the sleep of the enchanted.

I wouldn't have the patience for that. I'm as twitchy inside as this man is on the outside. I know I shouldn't long to go, but I do. I am useless here. Never any good when there's life and death on the line, I can't save this man. I couldn't save Snowflake's newborn kid. I didn't help Mama, either, did I, when she was suffering? When she sent me for help all those years ago?

"Go down the path," she'd said, "through the pasture, keep straight on it, over the little bridge, stay on the path through the forest, and . . ." She waved her hand for me to go. But I hadn't wanted to go, had I?

"Astri," Greta says, "you could go get help, and I could stay with Svaalberd."

"No!" I cry. "I'm not leaving you here alone with this madman!"

"Should I go for help, then?" she asks.

"No! You are too little to go off on your own like that."

"Then we'll wait until someone comes."

So we wait.

B ut no one comes.

Svaalberd's eyes still follow me, and I don't know whether to look or whether not to, for when I do, I see something I don't want to know. His eyes betray that he is not a goat, not a troll, nor devil, demon, or spirit. He is just a man, and he is suffering.

I shift my gaze to his shirt, to the drop of wax that's dried there on the front. It's a trivial thing compared with the other dirt and stains around it, but it's that drop of tallow that draws my eye and won't let go.

In the story of the bear-prince and the girl, the enchantment could be broken only when the tallow was washed out of the prince's shirt. Only then could the spell be broken.

If I could scrub that spot away, could we turn back time? Could we go back and back and back to when the shirt was clean, before the tallow dripped on it, before I rose from the bed that night on my foolish errand, before we walked through the deepening snow to get to his farm, before he came to get me, before Papa left, oh! before Mama died? Could we go all the way back, and everything could be different? Maybe Mama would not have had to die and then Papa would not have gone away and then Greta and I would not be sitting here watching the life seep out of this man.

It may be that I haven't liked him much, but that doesn't mean I want him to die!

But there's nothing I can do.

Only there *is*, isn't there? Perhaps you have been wondering when I will remember that there is a book of cures, remedies, and charms right in that sack.

I open it and take out the book.

"What's that?" Greta asks, reaching toward it.

"Don't touch it!" I cry, snatching it away. "This is a book of prodigious power."

"Pro-jid-juss?"

"It means a terrible much. With this book, little sister, you can conjure up and put down the devil and get him to do just what you command. These pages teach how to put out fire without water, find buried treasure, cure diseases, remove warts, turn back the attacks of snakes and dogs, and banish all kinds of pain."

"*You* can do all *that*?" Greta says.

"Well, you have to know how to read writing," I admit. "That might cause us a bit of trouble."

After a few moments Greta asks, "Aren't you going to open it?"

I nod, but hesitate. I'm thinking of things I've heard said: that those who possess the Black Book can go mad. Some have even done away with themselves. It's said that it can be dangerous even just to *listen* to the words from this book. And I'm fairly certain the parson would not approve.

But I only want to use it for good! Is it all right to use a bad thing for a good cause? I want to do what's right. But how can I, when I am faced with only impossible choices?

As I struggle with this, Svaalberd tries to rise but is seized by such a spasm that he nearly folds himself in two—his head flung back and his legs behind him, as if head and feet will touch behind his back. There's the crunching sound of bones breaking, a snap like the whole trunk of a tree cracking apart. He gasps, the air seems to catch in his throat, and then he's still.

G reta and I cling to each other, trembling. Finally she says, "I think he's dead."

"*Ja.*" I breathe in the word.

We stand like that for a moment, and then Greta says, "Now we must have a funeral."

"Funeral!"

"We can't carry him to a church, so we'll have to do it ourselves," says Greta. "Here."

"It's going to be pretty hard to bury him," I point out.

"We shall just have to cover him with moss," Greta says. And so we do. We pull up a nice thick blanket of moss, soft from the rain, and spread it over his body.

Then Greta takes some dirt in her tiny hand. "Almighty, everlasting God," she prays, "teach us to number our days, that we may get us a heart of wisdom. Amen." She tosses the dirt on the mossy grave. "Out of the dust art thou taken," she says. More dirt. "Unto dust shalt thou return." And a little more. "Out of the dust shalt thou rise again."

"That is pretty good, little sister," I say. "You could grow up to be a parson and wear a black cassock and a white ruff around your neck."

"That can't happen," she says, "because women can't be pastors."

"In America they can," I tell her. That's likely not true, but they say that women are treated with more respect in America, so who knows?

"Now it's your turn to say some scriptures," Greta says.

I recite the only scripture that comes to mind. "It is easier for a camel to pass through the eye of a needle than for a goatman to enter the kingdom of heaven. So, old Svaalberd, I'm not sure you're going to make it. Amen."

"Now the sermon," Greta says.

"You give the sermon," I suggest. "You know all the words, and in the right order, too."

"You should give the sermon because you knew him."

"I don't think I really knew him," I admit. "How much do we really know each other, when it comes down to it? He told me once about the *huldrefolk*, and about how we live side by side with them, and sometimes I wonder if maybe we're all *huldre* somehow, hidden from each other in ways we can only guess at. I know Svaalberd was a mean old man, but what made him thus? Did he have that hump as a youngster? That would make for a hard life, wouldn't it?"

"This is a very strange sermon," Greta says.

"Yes, I suppose it is," I agree. "But I've been thinking that although I didn't know Mr. Svaalberd, not really, nor did he know me, the strands of our lives are braided together somehow." I pause, and in that moment I see that so is all of life, braided together—this talkative brook speaks my thoughts; the thrush trills out the song of my heart. Were I to stand still long enough, roots would grow from the soles of my feet into the earth.

It makes me dizzy to consider it, but I feel suddenly how all things are woven together, all things seen and unseen, all things alive now and that once were, for generations back and generations to come, woven of a kind of golden thread that links me to Greta and both of us to this man, to everyone and everything forever right now, this moment, world without end, amen. Which is how I finish the sermon: "World without end, amen."

A Feast

nce we've tied the gunnysack to the saddle and settled ourselves on Dapple, we set off in a westerly direction.

After a while it begins to rain in earnest. Soon we are soaked to the bone and shivering. Steam rises off Dapple's flanks, and I can feel Greta's little bones clattering against me as she clings to my waist.

"There is something about a funeral that always makes a person hungry," I say, as we ride into a village.

Greta cranes her neck to look at the shops and fine houses passing by. "I don't remember riding through a village before," she says. "Shouldn't we be going back for Spinning Girl?"

"Wouldn't you like to get out of the rain and have something to eat before we ride all that way?" I suggest. "I've always wanted to eat in an inn, haven't you?"

"An inn?" Greta asks.

"It's a place where they serve whatever you ask for on a plate with a spoon and all," I explain. "You have only to give them a few coins in exchange. And if I'm not mistaken, this is an inn right here."

Dapple seems relieved to be led into a stable behind the

building. When he's settled, Greta and I go inside the inn, where we sit down at a table laid with a fine linen cloth. A stout woman comes and takes the tablecloth away. Maybe she doesn't care much for the puddles made from our dripping skirts and dripping hair. But when I plunk the bag of money on the table, oh, that's different, isn't it?

"What'll you have, my dears?" she asks, all sweetness.

And we dream up all kinds of fine things we've never eaten but only heard of: mutton chops with mint jelly, fish pudding and lamb cooked in cabbage, sweet buns stuffed with almond paste and fragrant with cardamom, cream porridge sprinkled all over with cinnamon. We each try a cup of coffee, too, though we soon have our fill of *that*.

"I've been wondering," I tell Greta. "What was it that killed old Svaalberd? Surely a couple of missing fingers or toes can't kill a person, or half the parish would be dead by now."

"I think he died of lockjaw," Greta says matter-of-factly. "Like Mr. Christiansen did after he had that wound in his leg."

Lockjaw? I had not thought of that, but there is sense to it. Old Mr. Christiansen *did* act the same strange way before he died. Like Svaalberd's, his wound got nasty-looking and his jaw locked up, so he got that strange sneer on his face. Then he started twitching and jerking, just like the goatman did.

Even so, that doesn't lessen my guilt. For if I hadn't chopped his fingers off, he wouldn't have had the wounds.

And if he hadn't had the wounds, maybe he wouldn't have gotten lockjaw. And if he hadn't gotten lockjaw, he wouldn't be dead.

The coffee turns even more bitter in my mouth, and I vow to be a better person from here on out. No more lying, thieving, or maiming of any kind.

"I have been wondering about something," Greta says, "and I want you to tell me the truth."

I brace myself for her question. What will I tell her about why and how Svaalberd really died? Or for that matter, any of the things she might well ask?

But instead of any of those questions, Greta says, "Was it really like that? About Papa and the seven-headed troll? Or were you maybe . . . stretching the story a bit?"

"Well, yes," I say, considering. "I suppose it's possible the troll had only three heads."

The innkeeper clears away all the dishes and bowls and spoons and then addresses us. "You two shouldn't be riding about at this hour," she scolds. "You'll be wanting a bed."

This is how Greta and I find ourselves in a bed fluffy with something other than straw for ticking, with a down coverlet that is as soft as a cloud, and everything is just as if we were the three princesses in the mountain-in-blue (before they were taken away by trolls and made to scratch their many heads, of course). Except now instead of three, we are only two.

Greta falls asleep right away, but perhaps the bed is too soft, the coverlet too warm, everything too fine for the likes of me.

I look at the dirty old gunnysack lying there on the floor by the bed. In that sack is old Svaalberd's gold, and in there, too, is the Black Book. I rise from the bed and tiptoe to the sack, reach inside, and pull out the book, blacker even than the night. Perhaps I should throw it away? I've heard that those who try such a thing find that it flies right back. The book can't be burned by any ordinary fire, so it's said. Once you own it, it's yours. In a way, it owns you.

In the morning, the innkeeper hands me a slip of paper with words and numbers written all over it.

When she sees me studying it, she says, "It'll be one kroner for your bed and two for your meals and five *skillings* to board your horse."

"That much?" I say, by way of saying something.

I take out the leather pouch and count out eight coins and put them on the counter.

The innkeeper frowns at the coins. She picks one up and looks at both sides. "This is the old money," she says. "Maybe you still use it up in the hills, but here in town we use the new money. It takes one hundred of your coins to make one of these." She pulls a coin out of her apron pocket and holds it up.

"No doubt I have some of those, too," I promise, pouring the contents of the pouch out on the counter.

The innkeeper picks out coin after coin. She counts out many, many of the *skillings* and shoves four coins back at me.

"But . . ." I stammer. "That can't be. That's all of it! That's all the money we have!"

"Well, then," she says. "You'd best go straight home."

"We're not doing anything of the kind," I say. "We're going to America."

"Well!" she exclaims, her whiskery eyebrows inchworming their way across her forehead. "You are in a conundrum," says she. When I squint at her, she explains that it means a puzzle—a bit of a pickle. "For you're going to need quite a lot more money than that! Not to mention the proper documents. Have you got your papers?"

"Papers?"

"You'll be needing your baptism certificate and so on," she says.

This is the first I've heard of baptism certificates, but I don't tell her that.

"We have what we need," is what I say.

She looks at me sadly and pushes two of the bigger coins back to me across the counter. "Use these coins wisely," she says. "They're only a trifle, but a mere trifle is often enough when luck is on your side."

We Come to a Church

Mary, Mary—

She sat

on the stair,

and prayed to Our Lord,

to make the rain stop;

over peaks,

over trees,

over all God's angels.

hat's a spell to stop rain," I tell Greta, as we ride along in the drizzle. "The goatman used to say it, and the rain always stopped."

"It really works?" Greta asks.

"Maybe not always right away," I explain. "But eventually, the rain always stopped when he said that. Anyway, we shan't need it when we get to America, because it never rains like this there."

"That sounds lovely," Greta says, sighing.

"All the time the sun is not shining here in Norway, it is shining in America. So for every day it's glum and cloudy here, that's a sunny day over there."

"It must be very sunny there, then, for here we never lack for gloomy days."

There is nothing to be said to that, for that is truth, and today is the gloomiest of all. So we ride for a bit in silence.

Well, not entirely in silence, for there's quite a bit of stomach rumbling to be heard. There's naught left in the sack except for crumbs, and those are mush.

"In America," I tell Greta, "there is so much to eat, all you have to do is reach out—like that—and pluck a plum or an apple off a tree. Cloudberries—everywhere! And not just for a handful of days or a week or two, but on and on and on, months and months of them."

"Mmmm." Greta sighs and snuggles closer to me.

"And cream! The grass has so much fat in it, it's all the cows give is cream. You only have to stir it once or twice and it's butter."

I don't mean to be lying, only exaggerating a little to keep Greta's mind off the rain. But she's believing me, I can tell, so it must be lying. But she's not thinking of her hunger anymore or how cold and wet and miserable we are, so is it wrong?

"Are we going back for Spinning Girl now?" Greta asks.

"About Spinning Girl there is a conundrum."

"A comumdrum?" Greta says.

"Conundrum," I correct her. "It means a knotty kind

121

of puzzle. One you can't think yourself out of, quite." We are in a pickle, Greta and me. We have nothing much in the way of money, I see that now. The treasure was no treasure at all, just the goatman's hard-earned money. Or Spinning Girl's hard-earned money from the yarn she spun, more like. And I squandered it all on a meal and a bed.

On the other hand . . . there's a horse under us, and a saddle, and there's a bridle, too, and *that's* nothing to sneeze at. Perhaps it's not *our* horse, but that's a trifle.

If we go back for Spinning Girl, though, we'll have her and no horse. If we have no horse, we'll be back to walking. If we go back to walking, we shan't reach the harbor before the ship leaves for America. And we'll have no money, nor anything worth selling when we get there, either. And then how will we buy our passage and our food and the like?

"But are we going back for Spinning Girl now?" Greta asks again.

I feel as if my insides are made of hard knots and pebbles, balls of sticky tallow, tangles of yarn, and lumps of ash. If we go back, then we go backward in time, and Greta and I will be milkmaids and serving girls forever, or married to smelly goat men, with no say in what we do or where we do it. In America, goat girls can become princesses or parsons, or whoever they want to be. I don't know if that is generally so, but that's the way it's going to be for Greta and me. And anyway, there's another problem. We're thieves, or at least I am, and could be considered a murderer besides, and there are laws against such things and prisons, too, and I suppose a prison wouldn't be much of an improvement over the goatman's farm.

I shift my weight on Dapple and sit up straight, feeling all these lumps and tangles and knots and stones align inside me and lock into place like armor. And then I say, "No, Greta. No, we are not."

I won't think about Spinning Girl's smile as she wove us golden crowns. I won't think about her laughter at playing what she thought was a game. I won't remember how she wiped the blood off my face and helped me clean the filth from my dress the day Svaalberd threw me in the mud or how she braided my hair in plain and fancy ways. And I will not think of our last embrace when I pinned Mama's brooch on her dress. I will tell myself, as I'm telling Greta, that "there's the perfect place for her. For wasn't the farmwife kind, and didn't she tell me how she had always wanted a daughter? And didn't they have plenty to eat? And didn't they get a fine bargain, too? Why, Spinning Girl will be more useful to them than a stable full of horses. For in exchange for their horse, they'll get as much fine yarn as they'll ever want. For didn't the farmwife admire her spinning, too?"

Greta is silent, and I think of how Papa used to say, "Sometimes silence is an answer."

The little brook we ride along chatters so much, there's hardly need for us to talk anyway.

✻✻✻✻✻

After we have ridden a little farther, we come upon a church.

"Astri," Greta says, "there's a church."

"Yes," I agree, "there's a church."

"And it's Sunday, too."

That is apparent by the sounds of many voices in the midst of a hymn.

"We can't stop now," I tell her.

"Wouldn't it be a terrible sin, though," Greta says, "to ride right past a church while Sunday services are going on and not stop?"

"We had plenty of church yesterday," I remind her. "We did scriptures, said a prayer; we had a sermon. What's left to do?"

"Let's go in," Greta says. "I need to seek forgiveness for something."

"You!" I exclaim. "What need have *you* for forgiveness?"

"We are none of us as we ought," she says, which raises my eyebrows, you can be sure.

"You go in, Greta." I glance at the church—at its sharp steeple piercing the sky, and its carved dragons leering down from the roof with their poisoned tongues. "I'll wait out here with Dapple."

A jagged spear of lightning rends the sky.

"Don't you think you'd be safer inside?" Greta asks.

No, I don't. The way I look at it, I'm just as likely to get struck by a bolt of lightning inside as out. So I shake my head and help her slide down off the horse.

In she trots, and out I stay. For a while I stand by the stream that runs by the church, watching the rain make circles in the water. Each drop is like a snag in a silk curtain. I've seen silk drapes and even snagged one once, so I know what I'm talking about. Here I stand, watching the silky water snagging over and over and over, and each time it repairs itself, smooth again—a smooth, black ribbon.

The snags in my heart are so tangled and deep, I feel them there, twisted little knots that can't be undone. I've stolen the gold and hacked off the fingers and snitched the soap and swiped the wedding food. I've lied to my own little sister and left Spinning Girl behind, and now I'm stealing the horse, saddle, and bridle from the farm boy who never did anything wrong except display a bit of greed.

Is it more wrong to steal from a guiltless person than from a bad one? Is it a worse sin to lie to my sweet sister than to steal from a cruel master? It hardly matters, for with one swing of my arm, with one downward swipe of the knife, I'm sure it matters not what else I do in life.

Still, I make a vow to tell the truth from here on out. I listen earnestly to the hymn being sung within, and inch closer to the door. Herein lies forgiveness, so they tell me.

It's not long, though, before I get to thinking how churches are also the places where records are kept. For instance, baptism records.

Soon I'm creeping around to the side door and into the small room behind the altar. Sure enough, there is a big book that I can see is stuffed with papers, all looking official as can be. Trouble is, I can't read, so I don't know which is which or who is who. I am scratching my head over this when a throat is cleared behind me.

I turn to regard the parson himself, regal in his cassock and ruff. I give him a little curtsy and say, "Hello, Pastor. I suppose I've grown since you last saw me, somewhere between twelve and fourteen years ago. But I've heard tell you never forget a soul in your parish, so I suppose you haven't forgotten me, either."

"Oh, no, certainly not," says the pastor, uncertainly. "But remind me of your parents."

"My mother died, and my papa went off to America," I tell him. There. That's the truth, at least.

"Ah, yes . . ." he says. I see him trying to think who that might be.

"And now Papa has sent for me to join him in America, and I'll be needing a document saying I was born in this parish. I'm sure you can provide me with my record of baptism."

"That may be, but I must warn you that this emigration fever is like a contagious disease! You should stay here and support yourself honestly."

"Aye, but my papa has sent for me," I tell him.

"Ah, yes," he says, opening the book. As he pages through the papers, he rattles on about how we should not believe everything we hear from America, and how it is neither the paradise nor the land of Canaan people dream about, while I nod and say "Aye" and "*Ja*" every so often.

In the meantime, Greta appears, no doubt looking for me.

"I know it's been a long while since I was last in church," I tell the pastor, winking at Greta, "but you know how terribly far up in the hills our place is, and the work that never ended. It was quite a journey to get to church, but my mother did it when I was born nonetheless, for she didn't want to put my soul at risk, not for anything. Oh, she always said you were the best parson in all the land, she did . . ."

As I speak, Greta casts a dark look my way.

The parson comes up with a piece of paper in his hand. "It must be a very long time since you've last been to church, so you'd better have a good look at this document to see if it's the right one." He shows it to me, and I purse my lips, studying it.

"Here's my name." I point to the words I think are a name. "There it is, the whole thing." I'm hoping he'll say what it is, and sure enough, he reads it off.

"Margit Anna Olafsdatter," says he.

"That sounds right," I say.

"And your father's name?" he asks me, clutching the paper close to his chest.

"Olaf . . ." I answer.

"That's his Christian name. And his surname?" he asks.

"Oh, he's not a *sir*," I tell the parson. "He's just an honest farmer . . ."

"Margit?" Greta says. "We'd best take our leave." She takes my hand and starts pulling me away.

"Say, now!" the parson barks, and you can be sure I snatch the paper from his fist as we go out. "I'm not at all sure—" he shouts at us.

But we are already on Dapple's back. I am already urging Dapple forward with my heels. And we are running—yes, finally running—now through the heather, now along a path. The whistling of wind fills our ears, and the jingle of Dapple's bridle, his hoofbeats, and his breathing, hard and fast, while I cling to him and Greta clings to me. Birds start up and fly, spinning and wheeling in the air above us. A river rushes alongside, tumbling over stones, running and running, down to the sea.

Trifles

In the story of the girl and the bear, the North Wind carried the girl east of the sun and west of the moon and set her down under a castle. It was there that her prince was being held captive by the troll with the nose three ells long.

"The girl in the story must have sat under that castle wondering how she would get in," I say to Greta, "just like us."

For here we sit on the waterfront, Greta and I, looking at the America ship. It's not far by rowboat, but as unattainable as a castle as far as we're concerned, for how are we to get aboard?

All along the waterfront people unload their wagons and pile up heaps of trunks and bundles and barrels, chests and boxes, casks, chickens, and children. There are plenty of families with gaggles of little children. The boy who came by the goat farm—I've seen him, too, with a lot of Hallingdalers, all jolly as can be. He doesn't recognize me, and I'd like to keep it that way. Oh, and there'll be a parson aboard, it looks like, and his wife. I'll have to steer clear of them, too, I suppose, if Greta and I ever get ourselves on board.

But even if we do, how will we ever manage?

I hold in my hand a list of provisions recommended for

one adult for ten to twelve weeks of sailing, which a kind soul
has read off to me:

—70 pounds of hard bread

—8 pounds of butter

—24 pounds of meat

—10 pounds of side pork

—1 small keg of herring

And then there are potatoes, rye and barley flour, dried
peas and pearl barley, sugar and coffee. At least we know we
can do without that *last* item!

Further, we are to bring along such things as a water pail,
a cooking pot, dishes, and eating utensils.

So far, we don't have any of these things.

"Well," I tell Greta, "the girl in the story got herself into the
castle, and all she had was a tablecloth, a flask, and scissors.
Only three things."

"They were magic things, though," Greta reminds me.
"All she had to do was say, 'Tablecloth, deck thyself with fine
things,' and the cloth would be covered with all the best things
to eat. She had a flask that never ran out of drink, and scissors
that clipped in the air, and everywhere they snipped, bits of
velvet and silk made themselves into fine clothes. Do we have
anything like that?"

"We have quite a few things," I tell her. "Many more than
three."

After an accounting of our things, we find that we have

—a horse, saddle, and bridle;

—a skein of well-spun yarn;

—a hairbrush;

—and a key.

"And we have another thing," Greta says. "Something I stole!"

"You? A thief?" I can't help being astounded. "What is it?"

"It's a book." Greta wiggles and, reaching up her skirt, pulls out a little book bound in blue cloth.

"Where did you get this?" I ask.

"Papa sent it," Greta goes on. "I think he sent it to us, but you know Aunt . . . She always thought everything should belong to her."

"A book!" I say. "Why would Papa send us a book?"

"I don't know, but Aunt was very interested in it, and she was very angry when it disappeared, too!" Greta says.

I turn the book over in my hand, open it, page through it. "Why?" I wonder.

Greta shrugs. "I don't know. But I heard Aunt speaking to Uncle about how they must keep the book themselves, and so . . . I stole it! That's why I wanted to stop at the church. To ask forgiveness."

"You hardly need forgiveness for stealing something that already belongs to you!" I tell her.

"To *us*, Astri!" she says. "It belongs to *us*."

"Well, we won't sell *this* book, that's sure!" I say. "Everything else, we sell."

We make quick work of selling the horse, saddle, and bridle, and I make sure we get paid in town money, too. With the money from that and with help from the birth certificate, I am able to buy my passage as Margit Anna Olafsdatter.

"Now you must call me 'Margit,'" I remind Greta. "Don't forget."

"Well, Margit," Greta says, "we have three things left. The yarn, the brush, and a key."

"A key that doesn't unlock anything," I say. "Nobody wants that!" Then I remember the coins. I jingle them in my pocket. "We do have a few coins!"

"We could buy something with them," Greta says.

I think of the innkeeper's admonishment to use the coins wisely. "They won't buy much," I tell Greta. "I have another idea. You take the yarn and see what you can get, and I'll see what I can do with this hairbrush."

So Greta trots off, and I sit down on one of the chests piled there at the waterfront and start brushing my hair. After a time comes a girl in nice clothes, and her cheeks all rosy and pink.

"Would you mind picking those up for me?" I ask her, pointing out some coins lying in the dirt.

"Where did these come from?" she asks.

"Why, from my hair, of course," I tell her.

"Your hair! How does that happen?"

"It's this brush, you see." I turn the brush so it catches the light. "It makes gold coins fall from your hair."

"Nay!" she exclaims, but turns around, presenting me with the back of her head. "Brush *my* hair with it!" she demands.

So I start to brush, and after a few strokes, what do you know? A couple of coins drop from her hair.

"Oh!" she cries, then spins around and plucks the coins off the ground. "But these are just ordinary *skillings*. These aren't worth chicken feathers!"

"Of course not!" I tell her. "You have to brush for quite a while before the really valuable stuff falls out."

"Let me try it!" she says.

"No," I tell her. "That's enough for now."

She fusses and pleads, and finally there's nothing for it but that she simply must have the brush. "What do you want for it?" she asks.

"Oh, it's not for sale," I tell her. "It's been in my family for ever so long."

She simply must have it, though.

I name a price. That won't do, she says, she has to save all her money for America. That's what her papa says. I ask who her papa is, and she points to a man on the wharf and says he's a fisherman.

133

Well, then, I tell her I'll trade it for a cask of herring, some smoked fish, a sack of dried peas, and a cooking pot.

✻✻✻✻

G reta returns, dragging a small chest behind her. Inside is a nice thick sheepskin and a large wheel of cheese.

"That was a good trade!" I have to admit.

"It was the gold in the yarn that convinced the housewife," she says with a wink.

So now we have some things. Other things . . . Well, there's the baker who has so much bread it can't be long before it goes moldy. A farmer who has so many potatoes he can't possibly keep track of them all. The very stout man who could do with a bit less butter, and the woman who is so fluttery she should not have another bite of tinned partridge. When they look away for a moment or turn their backs, Greta and I are there to lighten their loads.

Oh, it's just a trifle. A trifle here and a trifle there. But as we well know, a trifle can be enough when luck is on your side.

Still, we don't have Greta's passage. "We have one more thing we could sell," I say.

"No," Greta says. "We won't sell the magic book. For that is a book of projidjuss power, and once you learn to read it, there'll be no end of wonders wrought. Anyway," she says, "I have another idea."

✻✻✻✻

134

So here we are, two young girls, down on the wharf. Gulls screech and wheel; fishmongers call out their catch. Ships creak and groan as they pull against their heavy anchor lines, the ships' tackle clattering against the masts and yards.

There's the pounding and pattering of feet, clicking of heels, clip-clopping of horses' hooves, rattling of wagons coming and going.

Voices call out to one another with greetings or orders. A light but steady rain ticks against the cobblestones and the canvas awnings, taps against the clay roof tiles, and patters on the boxes and crates, sacks of potatoes, kegs of herring, kettles, pans, mattresses and sheepskins, and the dozens and dozens of chests and trunks lined up on the wharf, ready to be loaded onto the skiffs that will take these things out to the ship.

A chest is being hoisted onto a skiff when a sudden downpour halts all work for a moment. The passengers scurry under awnings or into nearby shops. Even the dockworkers and ships' crews stop working during the worst of the rain, covering their heads with oilcloths and dashing for cover.

As for one wee girl, no one takes much notice of her as she crouches behind, or between, or perhaps even *inside* one of the many trunks that line the wharf, waiting to be carried aboard.

III

The Columbus

The Winds

When the girl in the story went to find her bear-turned-prince, she had to ask each of the four winds to carry her, in order to get all the way to the castle that lay east of the sun and west of the moon. But the only one of the winds who had ever blown all that way was the North Wind. He had once blown an aspen leaf thither. After that, he'd been so tired that he couldn't make a puff of wind for many a day.

Still, he said to the girl, "If you really intend to go there, and you are not afraid to come with me, I will take you on my back."

Yes, she was willing. She must go there if it was possible, one way or another, and she wasn't a bit afraid, go how it would.

So the next morning, the North Wind puffed himself up and made himself so big and strong that he was terrible to look at. Away they went, at a terrific speed, as if they were going to the end of the world. The wind made such a hurricane that when they came out on the big sea, ships were wrecked by the hundreds. Still, onward they swept and on they tore, and no one could believe how far they went, and still farther out to sea, and eventually the North Wind became so weary that he drooped and drooped until at last he sank so low that the tops of the waves touched his heels.

"Are you afraid?" he asked the girl.

"No!" She wasn't.

As for me, I am too sick to be afraid, too sick to be homesick, too sick to remember the sadness I felt as the ship wove its way down the long fjord toward the sea and how we watched the blue hills and gleaming peaks recede, never again to see our homeland.

I've had enough time to think on this voyage, and all that thinking, combined with the motion of the sea, makes a big sickening mass of trouble in my stomach. The ship lurches; my stomach lurches; my soul lurches; and my sins come out my mouth and over the rail and into the sea.

I know that God is supposed to be everywhere, but there is no possible way He would follow us out here, to this truly godforsaken place. Between each swell, there is a trough, and at the bottom of the trough is hell, or near enough. There is no God down there, watching as I vomit over the side rail.

Still, somebody's here, for I feel a hand on my back. A soft hand making gentle circles. When I turn, the hand holds out a handkerchief, which I take.

"There, now," says a woman's voice. "It will pass. You'll get used to the motion. In the meantime, the crabs appreciate all the meals they're getting."

When I turn to thank the woman, who should it be but the parson's wife!

"It would be nice if we would get a favorable wind," she says. "But as we are not getting it, perhaps the Lord is exercising us in patience."

"And disciplining our impatience," I mumble.

She smiles and starts to leave. "Keep the handkerchief, my girl," she says, turning back. "When you are feeling better, there's something I'd like to ask you."

She knows, I think. *She knows everything.* She knows that although I paid only one person's passage, there are two of us. She knows that the sweet little girl who seems to be everybody's child, or no one's, is my sister and a stowaway, and the food we're eating is stolen, mostly. Maybe she knows I practically murdered my former master. She can probably tell all this just because she is the parson's wife. For if God is all-knowing and all-seeing, then the parson—and probably his wife as well—must be almost all-knowing and almost all-seeing.

✢✣✤✥✦

For a few days I am too sick to respond to her. As a steerage passenger, I spend my days between decks. Most of that time is spent on my bunk, which, along with Greta, I share with three other girls. All seems to be going along well enough, if you don't count the seasickness, when the girl with the pink cheeks with whom I traded herring for hairbrush starts brewing trouble.

First she plunks herself in front of me and turns her head sideways, so as to look me in the face.

"I've never got one gold coin out of my hair," she says.

"Keep trying," I tell her. "It doesn't work every time—"

"Maybe I'll tell my papa," she threatens.

"—or for everyone," I finish.

"Who is that little girl?" She points to Greta.

"How should I know?" I answer.

"Hmmpf!" she hmmpfs, and flounces away, her shiny hair bouncing on her back.

If anyone on this ship gets sold as a slave to the Turks, I hope it's her.

Now the girl approaches a woman who is rolling yarn into a ball. "Is that little girl there"—she points at Greta—"is she your little girl?"

The woman looks up and over at Greta. She can't help but smile—everybody loves Greta—but she shakes her head no. "I think she belongs to that family"—she points with her chin—"the one with all the girls."

So Little Miss Busybody trots over to the mother of *that*

family and raises the same question and gets the same sort of answer.

I watch her through the slits of my half-closed eyes, too weak to do anything. And what could I do about it anyway? If this girl with the well-brushed hair goes around to every mother on board and asks, "Is she your daughter?" and gets the same answer from every one of them, what will she do then?

T he days go on, with the north wind buffeting or the south wind sweeping up big nauseating swells, or the west wind trying to push the ship back from whence it came. It seems we have to be tossed every which way by each of the winds except the one we need. Finally, the right wind finds us, and our ship, the *Columbus*, moves westward, all sails filled.

We steerage passengers are allowed—even encouraged—to leave our cramped quarters and go up to the top deck. There, people cook, eat, sew, and play cards. Greta runs about in a cloud of towheaded children, disappearing into one family and another. She's so good with the babies and the youngest of the toddlers, always willing to hold, coddle, and comfort them, that no one minds her at all. Everyone just assumes she is the child of some other family.

From the upper deck we can look down on the lounge of the first-class passengers and watch them while they talk, do their needlepoint, smoke their pipes, and read books.

When she doesn't know I'm watching, I stare at the parson's wife as she reads. She seems to disappear into the pages—as if everything around her dissolves and she is transported into whatever world inhabits the pages of that book. It's not like watching the goatman read at all. With him it was all darting eyes and shouting. The page was not a place to disappear into but a wall to bounce one's voice off of. Watching the parson's wife read makes me wish I could read, too.

⁂

Since there's a genuine parson on board, on Sundays everyone goes up on deck for services.

Even though I've gotten over the worst of the seasickness, I've managed to be ill every Sunday so far. Today I am on deck but standing at the rail, well beyond the congregation, as usual. And, as usual, queasy.

All the passengers are there, seated in two rows, the women and girls on one side and the men and boys on the other. The minister really has to use his deep voice to be heard above the wind, which wants to snatch his voice away.

"Suddenly," he intones, "there came from heaven a sound as of the rushing of a mighty wind, and it filled all the house where they were sitting. And there appeared unto them tongues parting asunder, like as of fire; and it sat upon each one of them."

I cast my gaze off to the horizon, at the dark clouds massing there, crackling with lightning.

"And they were all filled with the Holy Spirit, and began to speak with other tongues as the Spirit gave them utterance," the pastor says. He is telling all about Pentecost, when the apostles were suddenly able to speak in all the regional languages. I suppose it would be like if suddenly a Hallingdaler could speak the Telemark dialect.

It could be a lucky thing if we were all instantly able to speak English, which is what the Americans speak, and which nobody on this ship so far as I can tell knows a speck of.

What if a wind like that came up right now? It's not hard to imagine, given what we've been through already. And what if tongues of fire sat upon us the way it happens in the scriptures? Nobody seems the least bit worried about it. The sun shines in all its splendor down on their brass buttons and filigree brooches, on the colorful embroidered borders on their dresses and their white linen sleeves. They all look so fine, and they all seem to belong there, in their makeshift church.

Me? I am the black sheep, the ugly duck, the one spotted piglet in a litter of pink ones.

The Halling Dance

oday it is the thumping that brings me above decks. *Bang! Thump, thump, whump.* It's feet, I can tell that, lots of feet, but what are they *doing*?

There'll be no rest for me, of that I can be sure, so at last I climb the companionway stairs, up.

On deck, all is piercing light and whirling color. The fiddler saws away at his fiddle. There's a fellow with an accordion. And the deck swirls with dancing bodies. Then the Halling men start their high-kicking dance. Someone holds a long pole with a hat dangling at the end of it, and one by one, the dancers try to kick it off. They whirl and twirl to the music, then leap in the air—so high you must squint against the sun to see their legs scissor out, their white shirtsleeves flashing.

No one can reach that hat—who could? It seems as high as the pennants fluttering on the mainmast. But then one of the young men steps forward and gives me a little nod, and I give him a glance back. It's the blond-haired boy who came by the goat farm.

He wouldn't recognize me now, would he? Now that I'm all cleaned up, hair washed, the bruises faded? Still, my heart beats two or three times out of rhythm.

Oh, he's very fine, he is. He struts about with his head held high and his chest thrown out like a rooster's. He's nimble, too. He turns; he spins; he flips. All the while his arms swing by his side, casual-like, as if it's nothing much to him.

Then he whirls, winding up like a top on a string, and flings himself high as a wheeling seabird. There he goes— heels over head—and off the hat flies and away it sails into the sky, then down to the sea.

Oh! That creates a ruckus! People race to the rail. The owner of the hat shouts orders to "Nab my hat!"

While everyone rushes to watch where the hat will go, the boy saunters over to me, smooths his hair, and smiles.

"Do I know you?" he says.

"No," I answer quickly.

"You seem familiar," he says.

"You've seen plenty like me, I don't doubt," I tell him.

"No, not like you," he says.

Maybe he means that as a compliment, I don't know. But I suppose he wants a compliment himself, so I say, "You seem to know that dance well enough."

"'Tisn't much," he laughs. "But now I've lost the postmaster his hat." The boy does an imitation of the squat little man racing after his hat, and I can't help but smile.

"There, now!" the lad says. "A smile becomes you. Or perhaps you become *you* when you smile."

"Whatever do you mean by *that*?" Maybe I snap a bit.

"I hardly know, myself," he says, all sheepish-like. "But wouldn't you like to dance?"

"Me? Nay!" I tell him. "I have mending to do." I show him the needle and length of thread I am holding—a gift from a kind woman so I can mend my stockings. The boy tips his head politely and goes back to his dance.

Now I suppose I'll have to avoid the parson's wife *and* the Halling boy. Well, I won't think about it. If I were to close my eyes, I could imagine myself home in the mountains, my back against a boulder, my bare feet in the warm sun, the dancers on the greensward, and none of that to worry about.

But that is useless daydreaming, so I bend to my task. I've barely got my needle through the first hole when I notice Greta standing over me. "What did you say to Bjørn that sent him away so fast?" she asks.

"Who's Bjørn?"

"The boy you were talking to. The Halling boy who danced so well. Don't you like him?"

"Why should I like him?"

"Why shouldn't you?" Greta asks. "He likes you."

"How do you know that?"

"Big sister, you are so foolish sometimes," Greta says. "Would it hurt to be just a little nice? Why don't you show the goodness in you?"

"There isn't any," I say.

"Pfft!" Greta says. "You're as full of goodness as a hive is of honey. Stop pretending it isn't so."

Surely she is the only person on the face of the earth who would say such a thing, I think, as she skips away to join the other children.

They are all munching on sandwiches, and the ship's chickens cluster around the children, clucking and receiving bits of bread from them. When a rooster plucks an entire sandwich out of one of the little girls' hands, she howls and cries while the others laugh.

"Oh! You bad rooster!" Greta scolds the bird. He is so surprised that he gives the little girl back the crust.

I laugh to see this, then turn to my darning. I don't suppose I need to explain how it is my stockings came to be so full of holes? After traipsing up and down the mountainsides where thorns tore them, cockleburs grabbed, branches poked, and stones ripped, there is plenty need of repair.

Here's a rip I made running back to the goatman's farm.

I am just putting my needle to the repair of it when who should come up to me but the girl with the glossy hair, hands on her hips. Grace, I've learned her name is.

"I still haven't got one gold coin from that brush you gave me," she says.

"Like I said, it doesn't work for everyone," I tell her.

"It doesn't work for *anyone*, more like," she says.

I shrug and offer to give her the herring cask back.

"Don't want it," she says.

I shrug again. There's no herring in it anymore anyway.

"I know that the little girl there"—she points to Greta—"is your sister."

"What makes you think that?"

"She's the only one on the whole ship toward whom you are kindly disposed."

"Maybe she's the only one on the ship who's kindly disposed toward me!" I exclaim. I suppose there is a fancier way of saying that, more the way the shiny-haired girl said it, but that's the best I can do.

"Maybe if you directed a little kindness toward others," she says, "they would return the kindness to you."

I have an urge to poke her in the eye with my needle. Instead, I jam the needle through the stocking and pull it back out again, stitching up an eye-sized hole.

The only way to get her to go away is to ignore her, so I put all my attention to my task, repairing the snag that I got climbing the birch tree.

I am thinking fondly on those days gone by, for although they were difficult and dangerous, I would prefer them to having this troublesome girl standing over me instructing me on how to behave. Or just standing there breathing with her mouth open, as she is doing now.

When I feel someone sitting down next to me, I steadfastly ignore it, until I feel a soft hand on my arm. I turn, and there is the parson's wife, smiling her good-natured smile and patting my hand with her own. I marvel at its softness. It's a hand that hasn't shoveled a lot of manure, that's certain. She's from a fine family that lives in a fine house and has servants to do that kind of work. The thin gold band around her finger is brand-new and shiny, with nary a scratch on it. She hasn't been married long.

"Margit, isn't it?" she says to me, and I nod, my heart in my throat. Here it comes: the question I've been dreading. Or the accusation. It's one thing to have a silly girl from steerage making accusations; it's quite another having a grown-up, first-class parson's wife raising questions. Another thing: I worry that she can see right down into my black soul. That she knows my every misdeed. And that I've carried a Black Book aboard, risking lives and limbs and immortal souls.

I consider making a dash for the rail, but the sea is calm. I doubt I can feign seasickness.

"It seems your stockings have had quite some little adventures," says she.

"I guess you could say so, ma'am," I answer.

"Now," she says, and I hold my breath. "My first question is: Do you think you might need spectacles?"

"What?" I gulp.

"For your eyes," she says. "To see better."

I look at her.

"You're holding your sewing so close to your eyes," she says. "It seems you don't see terribly well."

"I didn't know I was doing that."

"Well," she says, "you're probably used to it. Once you're in America, though, it would be a good idea to get your eyes examined. My sister recently got spectacles, and she says it made the world look like an entirely different place."

Was this what she wanted to talk to me about? I swallow and nod and hope that's all she wants.

But she goes on in a musing sort of way. "You and I are maybe a little bit alike," she says.

I doubt it, but I don't say anything.

She watches the dancing for a moment and then says, "It's strange, but there is this odd feature of my personality that almost always makes me sad when I'm surrounded by joy and cheerfulness. I often succeed in *appearing* cheerful. Once in a while I can even defeat the seriousness, to be happy with the happy. No, I don't mean to say 'happy'; I'm often happy, even though I'm serious. I would rather say 'cheerful with the cheerful.' Ah, well." She sighs and smiles at me. "I don't really know what I mean!"

What is funny, I think, is that I know what she means. Why, in the midst of merriment, do I so often feel as if I am not really part of it?

So far, I think, this conversation is going fairly well. But then she clears her throat, and I can tell she's going to get serious.

"Well!" she says. "What I really want to say is this." *Here it comes.* "I know you are alone, and if it would help you, that is, if you are seeking employment in America, I am in want of a maid. Would you be interested in such a position?"

A firebolt from heaven.

To be a maid for a fine lady! Imagine that! A fine, kind lady with soft hands and a gentle voice! Unlike Svaalberd in every conceivable way. In a real house with a wood floor, maybe. This would be a big step up!

"We can't pay much to start, and we'll have very little room to begin," she says.

What about Greta? I look across the deck, where she is rolling dried peas with the other children. I want us to stay together, but we haven't got a *skilling* between us. What am I going to do about that? How will I finance what might be quite

153

a journey to find Papa? I can't say no to the parson's wife, can I?

"You are giving it a mighty hard thinking-over!" the kind lady says.

"May I give you an answer tomorrow?" I ask.

"Of course!" she says, then, looking about, adds, "My, it's getting late."

Night has come on quickly. The dancers disperse. The children are shepherded downstairs. Except for the crew, the deck is soon empty. There is just enough light to see that in the case of my now-knotted, knobbly stockings, the old proverb is true: Sometimes the patch is worse than the hole.

The Pest

he next day dawns, and I do not have to give the parson's wife an answer.

The weather has worsened; the crew has closed the hatches to prevent the seas that slosh across the upper deck from flooding our space below. It makes the dark space even darker. And smellier.

Most people sit on the bunks that line both walls—five to a bunk. The passengers sit holding their heads, or retching into buckets. The exceptions are the fishermen, who are used to this kind of motion. They're trying to catch a barrel that's come loose from the ropes that are supposed to lash it to the wall. The thing rolls back and forth across the floor, banging into bunks while people leap out of its way and the fishermen give chase.

Days go by. And nights, although it's not always easy to tell one from the other. It's so dark and the stench is so bad that the crew won't come down here. After several days, the first mate pokes a long, flaming, tar-covered stick down the hatch. This seems to tamp down the smell somewhat. Adequate privies would do a lot more to control the smell than his tar stick. There is only one privy for 160 people, and the illness that people are suffering creates a lot of bodily waste. I'll say no more on that subject, except to say that sickness—*real* sickness—has arrived.

It sweeps through steerage like a black-winged creature, alighting on first one, then another. It strikes with fever, vomiting, diarrhea. The Pest, they call it. The Blue Death.

And there is no one to help us. There is no doctor on board, and those who aren't sick with the Pest are seasick. The captain and crew are too busy to tend to anyone, for the same reason the passengers are seasick: storms. Meantime, the fever leaps from one to the next to the next.

Greta goes about with a cool, damp cloth, applying it to hot foreheads and saying soft words. Meanwhile, I stand off to the side, wringing my hands, unable to help. My tongue doesn't find the words, sweet and soothing, the way Greta's does. I stay in the shadows, pressing the handkerchief the parson's wife gave me to my mouth. All the while knowing what lies at the bottom of our little bundle of belongings, yet doing nothing about it.

"Are you afraid?" the white bear asked the girl in the story.

No, she said, she wasn't.

But I am.

The Postmaster

The sickness and the foul weather ease up as if using the same calendar. On the upper deck I try to elbow my way to the stoves to cook the last of our barley, but since so many others are trying to do the same thing, it's quite a wait. So I take up my darning again, hoping to repair the mess I made of my stockings the last time I tried to mend them.

Waiting beside me, the little man who lost his hat overboard strikes up a conversation.

"From what valley do you come?" he asks, and I tell him. Then he asks who my parents are, and I tell him. Then he asks my name, and I pause.

"Margit . . ." I say, and watch as he purses his lips. "Though most people know me as Astri," I finish.

He claps his hands and says, "Nay!" and I say, "Aye."

"I handled mail from your father," he says. "I handled all the mail for the valley."

"Is that so?" I pull the needle through the stocking as casual as you please, while my heart ricochets around inside my chest—*ping-ping-ping*—as if within an empty vessel.

"Letters, like. Or packages. You must know this, as they

were all addressed to you. In care of your aunt and uncle, of course. Coming all the way from America! Tell me, what tidings did he send? Has he had good fortune there? Found a good place to farm? How is it going for him?"

"Surely you know yourself, if you handled the letters," I say.

"I don't read the letters, mind you. Certainly not!" he exclaims. "Oh, my, no! Not I. I noticed they were fat, that's all, as if—mind you, I don't know as they did—as if there might have been money inside. So I thought maybe your father is doing well over there, and wondered where he might have settled. You know, we're wanting to find a place ourselves—a place where the farming is good."

I stare at the little hole I am stitching, and it seems that through that hole I can see how it all played out: Papa sending the money for Greta and me to join him in America, and Aunt thinking she would just borrow it for a bit, just long enough to host a wedding fine enough to impress the neighbors. Oh, it will all pay off in the end, that's what she would tell Uncle. That's what she would think, all right.

"From whence did the letters come?" I ask the postmaster, calm as you please.

"Oh, my. I wrote some of the names down in case I got there myself one day. Thought I might look him up." He pulls out a slip of paper and rattles off a string of words that sound like nonsense. He might just as well be saying "Twigmuntus, Cowbelliantus, Perchnosias."

"I'll write them all down for you if you like," he says.

"I'd like that very much," I tell him.

And so he does, writes it all down in scritches and scratches, and this I study with knitted brow, a way of pretending to read that I learned from the goatman himself.

I thank him kindly, and as soon as the postman moves away, I race to find Greta.

The Black Book

Greta is in our bunk, her eyes closed.

"Little sister!" I whisper, forgetting to use her name as we had agreed. "Wake up! I have news. Good news!"

Even in this dim light I can see her face is flecked with pricks of perspiration. How pale it is!

"Are you seasick?" I whisper.

Greta's eyes flicker open, and I spring back. Her eyes are glazed and strangely bright. There is a kind of agony there that I did not ever want to see.

"Don't worry, Margit," she whispers, "I'll be—" She closes her eyes against pain or nausea—I don't know which.

I want to believe it is nothing, that it will pass. But I've seen enough of this kind of sickness now to know what is wrong with Greta. And so I kneel by the bunk and whisper prayer after prayer.

I beg: "Please, God in heaven, make her well. Here I am on bended knee."

I argue: "Why isn't it *me* that's sick? I should be the sick one. Why should Greta suffer, she who's never done one bad thing in her life?"

I bargain: "If You spare her, I will never do a bad thing again. Not one more lie shall pass my lips."

And finally, there's nothing left for me to do but hold the bowl while Greta vomits and vomits again and keeps vomiting though there is nothing left inside her. I smooth her hair and help her lie back on the bed, dab her brow and kiss her hot face. All the while feeling wild with the need to do something.

If I ever needed magic, I think, it is now. A potion. An elixir. The troll's ointment that heals all wounds.

And then I know what I have to do.

I go to our little chest of belongings and, with pounding heart, dig down until my fingers touch the cool cover of the Black Book. "I care not what happens to my immortal soul," I whisper, "if it will save little sister." With a glance at Greta for courage, I pull out the book and open it.

Lines, squiggles, slash marks, circular swirls. I know these make words. I can see there are words there. Maybe if I concentrate very, very hard, I'll be able to read them. Perhaps it will be like Pentecost—there'll be the rushing of wind, and tongues of fire will sit on my head, and I will be able to read. But the words and letters swim on the page—my eyes full of tears. I can't read. Even spectacles would not help.

Still, *someone* knows how to read. Someone here. I hide the book behind me and bellow over the shipboard noise. "Fellow passengers," I shout. "Who here knows how to read?"

A number of hands go up.

"Let me ask this: Who is not afraid? Not afraid to face anything? A wild horse. A mad bull. The crack of lightning. Or"—I feel the darkness rolling out of my heart and out of my mouth—"the devil himself."

I look around at the alarmed faces, at these people who wonder what kind of madness possesses me. Some of them bow their heads or look away. These I dismiss. To the others, the ones who return my gaze, I ask, "Who?" and stare into their eyes. I see fear, even just at my question. I look for eyes that show no fear: the blacksmith. He's not afraid of wild horses, for he knows how to deal with them. He thinks he's not afraid of the devil, but he can't know for sure. The Halling boy whose eyes are clear and honest: He looks at me frankly. Love has made him unafraid of anything. As I think that, I'm surprised that at this particular moment I should realize that he cares for me. And there, back in the corner, tucked so far back that she is almost entirely in shadow, is an old woman in a dark dress and shawl, a clay pipe clamped in her teeth. I don't remember seeing her before. But there she is, with those gleaming eyes.

One of these people will help me.

I hold up the book. A shudder runs along those present, as if a cold draft has passed through the decking.

"Where did you come by such a thing?" a woman hisses.

"It should be burned!" says another.

"No ordinary fire will burn it," calls a deep-voiced man. "It will jump right out of the flames."

"Pfft!" says a woman. "Rubbish! It's all rubbish!"

The blacksmith, who has lost his wife and little daughter to the Blue Death, steps forward and points his thick finger at me. "Why did you wait till now?" he says, narrowing his eyes. "Why didn't you bring it out when others were suffering?"

"I'm sorry," I whisper. "I was afraid. Like all of you. But you'll see! Whether you believe in it or not, when it's your loved one who falls ill, you'll beg for help from it, or from anything else that might do some good. And now my own Greta has fallen ill."

"The book should be kept, if it can help with the sickness," someone says.

Others are of a differing opinion. "No!" shouts someone else. "It could bring ruin on us all and should be destroyed!"

I stand my ground, holding out the book and pleading with every ounce of my being.

The blacksmith recedes to his spot. He has no reason to help me, since I didn't help him, and I don't expect it from him. Bjørn stands up. For a moment I fear he will actually take the book, but then the old woman approaches, bringing the shadows with her.

I hold the book out to her with both hands.

"If you want me to help you," she says, "you must first promise me something."

"I don't have anything!" I cry. "Bits of food. Scraps of clothing."

"It shouldn't be anything you have now," she says.

"What do you want? My future earnings?"

The old crone shakes her head.

"All my future worldly goods?"

Again, she shakes her head.

"What? What do you want me to promise? My firstborn?"

The old woman's eyes light up. "That will do." She takes the book in her gnarled hands and opens it. Her eyes dance along the page, although her twisted fingers can turn the pages only with difficulty.

I watch her—what a crazy old woman! "Fine," I say. Anyway, she'll be long gone before I have any babies.

Glancing at Greta, I see her skin has paled, her lips are now a dusky blue. I sink down next to her, stroking her arms, her face, and murmuring to her.

"You may call me Mor Kloster," the old woman says to me. "As for the girl, try to get her to take water, as much as she will."

"Water? That's the best you can come up with?"

"Do as I say," Mor Kloster snaps, "and quickly."

I fetch a cup of water and carry it back carefully. "Drink, sister mine," I urge, putting the cup to her lips.

Greta shakes her head. "I'm going to heaven to see Mama," she says.

"No, don't go," I beg. "Don't leave me."

"Someday we'll all be together."

"No, we won't." It gives me a pang to say it.

"You'll die, too, Astri, someday."

"Yes, but I don't suppose I'll be going to heaven."

"Where are you going to go, then?"

"I'm going to America!" I tell her.

"But where are you going to go when you die?" she asks.

"Then I'll go to . . . Soria Moria."

"That's where I'll go, then," Greta whispers. "Tell me how to get there."

Soria Moria

To get to Soria Moria, we have to go east of the sun and west of the moon. But that's a trifle for sturdy lasses like us," I begin. "We'll make it by lunchtime, and when we get there, oh! It will be splendid! The table laid with all the best kinds of food: lamb with cabbage and cream pudding and marzipan cake. Lingonberries and cloudberries, Greta, big bowlfuls! And the most delicious drink ever tasted. I have some here. Try it!"

I tip the cup of water to her lips, and she sips a little.

The old woman stirs and places a cool damp cloth on Greta's forehead. She's familiar now, somehow.

"Do I know you?" I ask.

And the crone says, "I'll not say no." Her eyes are wet stones set in her wrinkled face. At next glance they are as deep and dark as pools. I catch a glimpse of myself in them. Past the reflection, the well is deep.

"I visited your house when you were small, years before this one"—she points to Greta—"was born."

It comes to me: *the scrape of chairs on the floor of the house, and the rustle of skirts. Coffee being poured into cups; the cups placed on the table. It might have been an ordinary day but for the women's voices: hushed and intent.*

Behind the voices, the distant lowing of cows, the cry of a rooster, and inside the house, a child's ceaseless wailing. And the old woman sitting at the hearth, heating something over the fire.

"Your mother said she had done everything right," Mor Kloster tells me now. "Or at least as right as she could do. 'Not a thing forgotten, back when you and your twin were newborns,' said she. She put a pair of sheep shears in the cradles, consecrated the babes' wash water, made the sign of the cross. She never neglected to say 'In Jesus's name,' not once in the important places.

"'See you there?' said your mama, and pointed to the lintel above the door where she had stuck a knife into the wooden beam. 'There's steel,' she said. But then there'd been the question of silver, and she only had but the one brooch. She could only pin it on one of the babes' dresses, couldn't she?"

The old woman looks up at me. "She had to choose, you see. Oh, both babes were healthy to start—that's the way it is. But then something changes. Somewhere along the way a healthy babe turns into a monstrous thing.

"'Why?' your mother asked, pointing to the healthy toddler. 'Why has this one all the health? Oh, she's as sturdy as a fjord pony,' she said, 'while the other child lies in bed day and night howling till its face is purple as a turnip. And look at it!'

167

"The children were toddlers by the time I was called in, and one of them was a strange one, all right, with soft bones and nothing for joints but jelly. Her legs bowed like a sheep's, her head thick as a cabbage. And there she lay, not up and running about but whimpering and wailing by turns."

I remember now. I remember a voice coming from a dark corner. "I shouldn't wonder," *the voice addressed Mama,* "if the huldrefolk, seeing you have more babies than you can care for"— *here the woman in the corner had lowered her voice to a terrible low whisper—"if they didn't steal your child and leave one of their own behind."*

"Oh, that was a woman without a heart in her body," Mor Kloster says. "I shot her a dark look, you can be sure, but she just sat with her eyes on her knitting. And your mama turned away, biting her lip. I melted the lead over the fire. Good lead, it was, too, scraped from church windows at the seam of the year."

I remember watching as the old woman lifted the beaker from the fire and carried it to the little bed, then poured the melted lead, hissing and sputtering, into a waiting bowl of water, which she held over the child's head. "I heal you in the name of God the Father, God the Son, and God the Holy Ghost for nine kinds of* svekk *and nine kinds of English disease. Peace be with you.* I Jesu navn, *amen," the old woman had prayed then, staring into the bowl.*

Or perhaps she has said that just now.

The ship pitches suddenly, and I worry that the hot lead will spill on Greta, then realize where I am: in the gloom of between decks, and that same old woman, older now, of course, reaches over Greta to pat my hand.

"It's so long ago now, I can't remember how it all turned out," she says. "Which one of the babes were you?"

I cannot clearly see myself. Was I the one whimpering in the bed? Or was I the one toddling about the room? The healthy one or the sickly one? The human one or the changeling?

"Your mama had her hands full with two, especially since one was sickly," Mor tells me as she squeezes a little water from a cloth into Greta's mouth. "So your papa took the healthy one with him when he could."

Now I remember that Papa would plunk me in a puddle of sunshine while he went about his work.

"Somehow," Mor Kloster says, "that one got pinker and stronger while the other babe at home grew puffy and weak. Your mama got the blame; it was said she did this or that wrong. Your aunt went so far as to claim that the *huldrefolk* had exchanged the child for one of their own. Something should be done about it, she'd said."

And Mama had done something.

Greta coughs weakly and says, "Tell me how to get there, big sister, to Soria Moria, so I can find you."

"There is a path," I begin again, "along a mountainside." As I tell her, I remember that I had to walk, but Mama carried the other child.

"We walk along, walk along," I tell Greta, "with the valley below and the mountains rising on each side."

It had been a gloomy day. "Most likely it is a gloomy day," I say, "as dark outside as it is in this dingy place." *The mountains were shrouded in dark and shifting shadows: the hills rolling away, smudges of purple, their rocky edges black under the glowering sky. But across the dale, on the mountainside, the sun was shining in one spot and nowhere else. And that one spot was lit as if made of gold, a brilliant sparkling patch of light.*

"Do you see it, my girls?" Mama had said. "That's where we're going. It is Soria Moria, where everything is as good as good can be and there is so much joy, there is no end to it."

And I guess I have just said it myself, for now Greta's eyes close as if satisfied.

She sleeps; she drifts; she swims away from me.

"Don't go!" I whisper. "Don't leave me behind."

So that's how it was that day long ago. There were three of us who went to Soria Moria, but only two came back.

Astri's Dream

I lost one sister, I realize now. I cannot, *will* not, lose another. I'll do anything—anything!—to save Greta.

But things begin to spin. Everything turns and turns as if I am dancing with the Halling boy, everything whirling. Then all goes dark.

When I open my eyes again, there is a revolving swirl of colors, people's faces; the familiar look of the bottom of the upper bunk passes by. I squeeze my eyes shut against it all, but behind my closed eyes is a rush of color and everything spinning, even though I know I am lying still. I hear distant voices, the muttering of incantations, the whisper of fabric, the milkmaids calling the cows from a distant hillside. The smell is the worst of it, though—the horrible stench of trolls, trolls with more heads of greasy hair than I can count.

The bed starts to sink, and down it goes, through the decking to the lower hold, through the bottom of the ship, through water, then through fire, and Astri finds herself back in Norway, running along a grassy hillside. Wreaths of mist cling to the mountains while little brooks rush and sing down the slopes. Astri runs and runs, startling birds that swoop and fly overhead, past a herd of reindeer who raise their heads as she passes. One bolts, and the entire herd runs with her, running and running to Soria Moria.

Finally, she comes to a castle where she walks through the dim halls, with torches glimmering and sooty shadows on the walls. A whirring sound draws her toward a chamber, but when she tries to go in, she finds it locked. She takes the key from around her neck and unlocks the door. On one wall hangs a great, gleaming sword, and next to it, a leather drinking flask. Beneath it, a girl sits spinning golden thread. The girl turns toward her, and at first Astri thinks it is her own self she confronts, as if in a mirror. But then she recognizes that it is not herself but her twin, a silver brooch glimmering on her dress. In the same instant, she realizes it is Spinning Girl.

They stare at each other for a long moment, and the girl says nothing, but still Astri hears her words. "You'd best get out of here as fast as you can, for soon the troll will be home. And he is a three-headed monster."

"I'll stay here and fight the troll," Astri says, catching the rancid, old-man smell of the troll and his many greasy heads. "I don't care if he has twelve heads! I'll chop them all off! Just let me have a drink from that flask."

"You want his flask?" the girl asks. "I'll let you have it on one condition: that you leave right away."

"But then I can't save you," Astri says.

"I can take care of the troll myself," says the girl. "Now, listen to me. Outside this castle there is a mountain. You will have to climb *that mountain to get to the castle that lies east of the sun and west of the moon."*

So Astri slings the strap of the flask over her shoulder, casts one glance at Spinning Girl, and out she goes. The mountainside is as steep as a wall, and so high and so wide that no end could she see. Nonetheless, Astri starts up the steep rock with the flask slung over her shoulder.

Midway up, she comes to a small ledge where a man sits.

"Don't you want to stop and share a drink out of that flask you're carrying?" says the man.

"What sort of man are you, and from whence do you come?" Astri asks.

"I am your Father from heaven," the man says.

"Oh, no," Astri says. "I will not drink with you, for what I know of fathers and their like is abandonment, abuse, and neglect. Oh, maybe you're not like the rest, but I'll not drink with you all the same." And on she climbs.

After a time, she comes to another ledge, where another man sits and asks her the same question. This time the man claims to be the devil, come from hell.

"I'll not drink with you!" Astri says. "I've had enough dealings with you already."

Off she sets again, until she comes to another ledge, where there sits a man in a slouch hat. He seems familiar, and she asks, "Do I know you?"

"You've had dealings with me," says the man. "They call me Death."

"You, I'll drink with," Astri says, climbing onto the ledge. She hands him the flask. "Because I have some questions. First of all, I want to know what you plan to do about my little sister."

Death takes a long drink, while Astri goes on. "I understand that people can't go on living forever," she says, taking the flask from him. "But tell me, what's the use of taking a little child who's not been on earth long enough to harm a single soul and is so full of goodness she'd have spread it around her like flour from a torn sack on a windy day?"

"There's no sense to it, I don't suppose," Death says, "but let's have another sip from that flask."

She hands it back and says, "That's all you have to say—that there's no sense to it?"

"Perhaps you should climb back down the mountain to that other ledge where our Father in heaven was sitting and ask him," Death suggests.

Astri cranes her neck to look over the ledge down the sheer cliff face. "I suppose he'll say the same thing our parson would say: 'She's going to a better place. She's going to join her mama in heaven. A place without suffering. Without hardship. Without illness. Without death.'" Here Astri glances at Death, who's in the midst of another swig.

"That all sounds very nice," Death says.

"Nice for her!" Astri cries. "What about me?*" She squeezes her eyes shut for a long moment, realizing what she has just said. With her eyes closed, she senses a rocking motion. In her ears, the distant sound of voices, footsteps, the creaking of ship timbers, the clattering of tackle, wind.*

"I have a bargain." Astri opens her eyes and turns to Death, who is holding the flask to his lips. "Why don't you take me instead?"

"I'm trying to," Death says, taking a long drink.

"So"—it begins to dawn on Astri—"that's what is happening? I am dying? Or am I already dead? Or am I dreaming?" It doesn't matter which it is, she thinks. She has to finish what she set out to do. "Listen," Astri offers. "You can take me—I'll go willingly, straightaway—if you promise not to touch Greta."

"It doesn't work like that," Death says.

"Can I pay Greta's way out? I don't have any money, but I know where I can get a silver brooch."

"No," says Death. "I don't take bribes."

"What about love? What if I just love her so much she cannot die?"

"Love is very powerful," Death says.

"Yes . . . ?"

"It can accomplish much," he says.

"Go on," Astri urges.

"But even love cannot stave off death. There is no way you can stop it if it's destined to happen. But I'll tell you what: Since you have

been so generous as to share your drink, I will give you a gift: If you go into a sick person's room, you will be able to see me. If I am sitting at the feet of the person, then that means that person can be saved—maybe with that water you have in this flask—but if I am sitting at that person's head, then neither medicine nor magic are of any use, for that person belongs to me."

"So that's my gift?" Astri asks. "That I can see you? I can see Death? It seems a dubious talent."

"Maybe so," Death says. "But you never know what might come in handy in a tight spot. Just remember, no one has ever been able to change the outcome."

Death tips the flask back as if to drain the last drop, and Astri snatches it away from him and flings herself on the rock wall and scrambles to the top.

At the top, she starts running, over mountain and moor, shoes tap-tapping along the rocky ground, whispering over moss, through snow, until a big wind picks her up and carries her through fall, then winter, then spring. Leaves fly past, then swirling snow, sunshine, and rain. Is it the wind or a cantering horse she rides, the silver buckles on its bridle jingling and its leather saddle creaking, and the wind pushing the pine boughs so they sound like the crashing of waves?

"Do you see something?" the wind asks.

"I see something a long, long way off," Astri says. "It's sparkling and twinkling like a tiny star."

They journey on, through many a land, through forest and field, and then the wind asks, "Do you see anything now?"

"Yes," Astri says. "Now I see something a long way off, shining like the moon."

"Look at me," the moon says, and the wind canters on, silver buckles jingling, leather saddle creaking, and the pine boughs sounding like the crash of waves.

The moon prods and prods . . . "Open your eyes," the moon says. "Look at me."

I open my eyes.

M or Kloster's face hovers above me, round and glowing as the moon.

"My girl!" she exclaims. "I thought we had lost you!"

"Where is Greta?" My eyes follow the old woman's to where Greta lies on the bunk next to me.

I raise myself up on one elbow to look at her. She is so still, so very still.

"Is she . . . ?" I ask.

"She seems to be neither here nor there, but somewhere in between," Mor Kloster says.

There are many people clustered around our bed: the stout farmer from whom we stole a ham; the fluttery woman who, it seemed, had more tinned partridge than she needed; the baker whose quantity of bread would surely have molded, had I not reduced it; the mothers of children with whom Greta played; and the children themselves. And then I see the old fellow in the slouch hat: Death. He is sitting right next to Greta's head, and my heart grows cold.

Death is dozing and nodding his head. Perhaps all that drinking made him drowsy, I think, then remember that was in my dream. But so was Death in my dream, and here he is, sitting by Greta's head, half asleep.

Asleep!

When his chin next drops to his chest, I sit up and whisper to those present, "Spin her around! Turn her so her head faces the other direction!"

They look at Mor Kloster. "Why not?" she seems to say, with a shrug and a nod. The others lift Greta and turn her around in the bed so her head faces the other way. Mor hands me a cup of water, the same little cup that I carried from the barrel for her—it might be days ago by now, as far as I know—and I reach over and put it to Greta's lips.

No sooner have I done this than the old fellow wakes up and looks straight at me. Oh! He's angry when he sees what I have done. He stalks around to my side of the bunk and hisses into my ear. "Now you've cheated me!" he says. "And now I will have to take *you*!"

I thought I was ready for this. I thought I'd say, "That's all well and fine. I'm ready to go." But it seems that now that I can see Death, I can also see Life. I see it in all those faces around the bed. I hear it in the soft—sweet!—murmur of voices, in the water talking along the sides of the ship, in the thrum of life around me. I feel it in this close, warm space, filled with the smells of cooking grease and wet wool socks, a leaky herring cask, sour milk, and musty trunks. A lantern makes a warm yellow puddle of light nearby. It seems I can even see the golden thread that stitches us all together, making a kind of wreath that encircles us all. It's Life, and I don't want to leave it. Besides, who will look after Greta if not me? And furthermore, I don't want to go.

Still, "a bargain is a bargain," I tell Death. "I'll go with you. But surely you'll let me say the Lord's Prayer first. Then, as soon as I'm finished, you can take me."

He sighs and says, "All right. Get to it."

I lie down, pull the covers up under my chin, fold my hands on my chest, and close my eyes. "Our Father," I begin, but I don't finish. It seems I've fallen asleep.

Grace

What brought her back to life?" I ask Mor Kloster. Greta is sitting up in bed, drinking broth. "Was it a spell you said? Something from the Black Book? Was it the water I gave her? The dream I had . . . *Was* it a dream?"

"Perhaps it was little bits of all those things," Mor says. "Mostly, I think it was what it usually is in these cases: grace."

"Grace?" I look down the length of the ship to where Grace is playing quietly with one of the babies.

Mor laughs. "No," she says, "not Grace, may she someday grow into her name. I mean the grace of God. A gift, even though we may be undeserving."

"Like a golden spinning wheel or a golden carding comb."

Mor glances over at me. "That is one way of looking at it, I suppose," she says.

I want to tell Mor about my dream, but as it's a dream, it's hard to explain. And I can only remember wisps of it. Wisps and shreds, like fog that swirls in and settles, then lifts. And then I remember about Soria Moria, and Mama taking us there.

"I dreamed of my sister," I tell Mor. "I left her, too, just like

Mama did. How could my mother have left her behind like that? My twin! How could she?"

"She left the child for the trolls to take in exchange for her real daughter. But when she went back, the child was gone and no other to take her place!"

The goatman, I think. He found her and took her.

"I left her, too," I tell Mor, "in Norway. I didn't know she was my sister!"

"In your life you will have many sisters," Mor Kloster says, but before she can say anything else, the first mate comes clattering down the companionway stairs and stands in front of us. He has to hunch a little because he is so tall. It is clear from his face that he can't wait to get back above decks as soon as possible. But he takes off his cap and says, "It has recently been brought to our attention that there is a passenger who is aboard illegally."

Everyone goes quiet. The passengers avert their eyes, stare at the floor, look anywhere but at Greta.

And sure enough, here comes Grace, pushing her way through the crowd. I expect to hear her crow and see her strut about, proud of herself, but she quietly tugs on the first mate's shirtsleeve until he looks down.

"The little girl I told you was a stowaway," she says, "well . . . you see . . ."

Grace steps aside, and the blacksmith steps forward,

clears his throat, and finishes her sentence. "She's mine," he says. "She's my daughter."

Hands fly to hearts. The first mate looks around at the faces, squints one-eyed at the blacksmith, who stares back at him with a look that might have been forged in one of his hottest fires. The mate runs his fingers through his hair, puts his cap back on, and wordlessly retreats up the companionway stairs.

Then the blacksmith goes to the edge of the bed and takes Greta's tiny hand in his great big one. "I have room for you in my home"—his voice cracks a little as he says this, which sends the women nearby scrambling for their handkerchiefs—"and in my heart," he finishes.

Now everyone is sniffling. Everyone except me. I feel like I have an iron plate in my back. Have I gone three days past the end of the world to save Greta only to lose her to the blacksmith? Oh, I realize he can give her a home, and what can I give her?

Nothing.

He says nothing to me.

I say nothing back.

Is life just a series of losing people? I wonder. First Mama, then Papa, then a sister I didn't know I had, and now Greta, my last and best treasure. It seems that instead of gathering my family together, I have lost them all, one by one.

But what can I do? Our food stores are gone. What little money we had is gone. We really have nothing at all. I know that it's best if she goes with the blacksmith and I go off to the parsonage.

"It won't be forever," Greta says after everyone has drifted away.

"I know," I say, and try to smile, but like the troll caught out in the daylight, I feel myself turning to stone.

⁜⋆⋆⋆⁜

D ays pass while Greta stays in bed, gathering strength. As for me, I'm strong enough to go above decks, where I sit at my spot against the mizzenmast. It is so still today that I have watched as the ship went all the way around in a circle and is now on its second pass. Not the slightest breath of wind comes through the air.

Just like me: out of wind, as listless as these drooping sails.

I should be happy, I suppose. Everything has worked out. I have accepted the parson's wife's offer. Now Greta has a home, too. She and I won't be all that far from each other, as it turns out, so we'll be able to see each other now and again. I remember the parson's wife saying how she was oddly never happy when she was supposed to be, and I think, well, maybe we *are* alike. Because although I suppose I should be, I'm not happy.

"It's the remnants of the illness," Mor says, but I am not so sure about that. I feel that I am made of nothing but knots and tangles, hard stones, steel plates, and icy cold water. That's all there is, and when I am not having to press the weight of all

183

that against something difficult, there isn't much of me.

I look out at the ocean, stretching in all directions like the marble floors of Soria Moria castle. The ship is like the forgotten toy of a giant's child, carelessly left behind.

I stare at that marble ocean and say, "I could walk on that, I don't doubt."

A voice behind me says, "No you couldn't." I turn to see Bjørn, who says, "Come with me."

"What do you want?"

"I don't want anything," he says. "Mor Kloster sent me to fetch you. She wants your help."

"Help with what?"

"There's a baby wants birthing."

"I don't know anything about that," I tell him.

"Mor Kloster says you are the one she needs," Bjørn insists.

"There are others better suited to that sort of task," I sniff.

"Are you afraid?" he asks.

I look at him, and he returns my gaze, steady. "I'm not afraid," I say and hoist myself up, then follow him into the dim recesses belowdecks.

"She's in there," Bjørn says, pointing.

Someone has hung quilts around the bed for privacy, but they can't keep out the screams. My hand goes to my chest, where my fingers find the key that hangs there. I clutch it with one hand while pushing open the drapes with the other.

Inside the cloth walls it's even darker and warmer, and it doesn't smell too sweet, either. The mother-to-be is writhing on the bed, her pale face glistening with sweat, her hair as wet as if a bucket of water had been poured over it. Her eyes flick from face to face, begging for help. They lock on mine just as Mor grabs my arm and pulls me in.

"I can't help you," I say.

The old crone holds up her knotted, swollen hands. Then she takes mine and holds them in front of my face.

"Look at those fine hands, my girl. Small and smooth and deft. Those hands our good Lord gave you. Shouldn't you be making use of them?"

"I *have* made use of them," I mumble.

"*Good* use, then," the old woman says, catching my eyes with hers.

She knows all, I see.

"There are things that need doing that I cannot do, but for which you are well-suited—" She goes on talking, but I stop listening, for who should be sitting at the foot of the bunk but the old gentleman in the hat: Death.

He shoots me a dark look, and I bolt for the curtain. But Mor Kloster is fast for an old lady, and she grabs me before I can get out.

She explains what she wants me to do as she plunges my

hands into a bowl of warm water and hands me a slip of soap. The baby is going to come out feet first, she tells me, handing me a towel to dry my hands, and is going to need some help. "Quickly," she adds.

Well. I've done other hard things, haven't I? And wasn't I just wishing for something difficult to have to press my weight against?

So I find myself kneeling on the bed, trying to get in some better position, if there is such a thing, for this task. I give Death a wary glance, and he raises an eyebrow at me.

"Water . . ." the woman on the bed whispers, and I remember Mama whispering in the same harsh-throated way. I was only five when Mama gave birth to Greta. Papa was out in the forest, and it was just Mama and me at home.

I brought her a cup of water, then stood with my fingers in my mouth watching for a while. She was suffering, I could see that. Her eyes squeezed shut against the pain, her hair matted, her skin clammy. Mama didn't seem like my smooth-faced mother anymore, the mother who took care of me, sang lullabies, and kissed my bruises.

"Astri," Mama said, "I need you to go get help. Go get Mor Kloster. You know how to get there. We've been there together. Go down the path, through the pasture, keep straight on it, over the little bridge, stay on the path through the forest, and . . ." She waved her hand for me to go.

I ran out of the house and down the path. I knew the old crone who had come to our house in her dark skirts and hushed voice. She was a scary old woman. Maybe a witch! She smelled of camphor, and her eyes were black as a mink's.

My steps slowed.

But then I thought of Mama with her damp skin, her tangled hair, her stifled cries. She thought the troll kone *could help her, and so maybe I should fetch her as Mama had asked.*

The legs and baby's bottom have emerged, and Mor Kloster tells me that the babe's arms need to be released from their crossed position before the baby can be fully born. I am supposed to reach inside and do this.

I feel my hands being guided, as Mor whispers in my ear. "Very fine," she says.

The mother groans.

"Don't let her move," Mor Kloster says, and the other women place their hands firmly on the woman's shoulders and legs.

I scampered down the path, through the forest, and out into the open heath. It seemed to me that after the old woman had been to our house the first time, everything had changed. Mama stopped singing. She cried sometimes when she thought no one was listening. She stared out windows. And she had stopped loving me.

I plopped down in the heather to think. After a moment I lay down and looked up at the clouds moving across the sky in a regal parade. There was the King of the Clouds, and there the Queen. Next came the princesses, a dozen of them, in their fluffy pink dresses. For a while I lay like this, watching the clouds float by. But then I began to feel that perhaps the ground was moving and the clouds were standing still. The more I thought about it, the more that seemed to be how it was, and pretty soon I felt the earth speeding along so fast I had to hang on for dear life. I stretched out my arms and clung to the grass and stones under my fingers.

It made me dizzy, thinking how fast the earth was hurtling along, and where were we going? I wondered, closing my eyes.

After a while of the world spinning like this, I heard a clucking sound, and I opened my eyes. There, standing over me, blocking the clouds from view, was the old troll hag herself!

"Here's a tender little mushroom, ready for picking!" the old crone said.

I scrambled up. "I'm not a mushroom!" I said. "I'm a girl."

"A little girl, are you?" said the woman. "What are you doing out here all by yourself, then? Where's your mama?"

Mama! I was filled with shame when I remembered my mother at home, suffering. Somehow I had lain down in the grass and watched the clouds go by instead of fetching the old lady as I had been told. "Mama wants you to come," I said. "Hurry!"

"There's trouble?"

I nodded.

"Why didn't you come for me right away? Why was it I found you here, lying in the meadow, gazing at the sky?"

"I was afraid . . ."

The old woman took my hand in her own and set off down the path.

"It can be a fearful thing to meet your destiny."

Did she say that then, or is she saying that now? I wonder, as with my fingers I move the tiny arms across the babe's chest.

"Well done," Mor Kloster whispers in my ear. "Now, gently . . . gently . . ."

In the next push the child is delivered, slippery and red-faced and very much alive. And for a moment, I am back in the cotter's hut with Mama, and Greta is delivered in the same way, all shiny and goopy and screaming her head off. I remember this, and that there was so much joy there was no end to it. Except it did end, quickly and harshly, for Mama died then, not long after. And that was when a cloud passed over the sun, casting a dark shadow that never moved away.

"Hand the child to me," says Mor.

I realize I am holding the infant; the pulse and thrum of its life courses through my hands and into my whole self. Or perhaps that's me, trembling.

"Now you have fulfilled your part of the bargain," Mor Kloster says to me.

"Bargain?"

"You have delivered to me your first born. No doubt you will help birth many more in your years." The old woman says this as she is inspecting the babe. Then she glances up, and our eyes meet. She gives me a little nod, and the other ladies in the makeshift room laugh.

"'Tis her first born, that's so!" one says, and they are all a-chatter about it and wasn't that a clever thing, and hadn't they been wondering how it was going to turn out after all?

Mor instructs me how to swaddle the infant, placing the child's arms across his chest and wrapping the band around the babe. I'm to wind it in a special way and tie the band so it forms a cross. But I'm trembling so much I can't do it.

"Steady . . . steady," Mor says, her words themselves steadying me. And the trembling starts to feel like . . . well, like thrumming. Like the whirring of Spinning Girl's wheel. It seems to shake loose the knots and knobby bits and stones and steel inside me. All those hard bits soften and dissolve a little, like lead in a beaker, slowly melting over a warm fire. It's scary and daunting, but exciting, too. Is this how it feels to meet your destiny? I wonder.

"Let us say together the Lord's Prayer," says one of the women.

I bow my head and part my lips, and then I remember! Death is there, just waiting for me to utter the words of the prayer. If I say it, he'll have me. So, as the first words are spoken, I pass the babe to his mother, duck outside the curtained walls, and gulp down some air. My heart buzzes with the words, but not a sound escapes my lips.

When the women bustle off to make "bed food" for the new mother, I step back into the chamber. I glance at the place where Death sat, but he has gone. On to the next soul, I suppose. Or perhaps he was never there at all.

Mor hands me the Black Book. "Here is your book," she says.

I back away.

"It's just a book," she says. "You might find some useful thing in it, now and again. There are cures there, but there's plenty of rubbish, too."

"How do you know which is which?" I ask her.

"That comes from practice. And from using this"—she points to her head—"which you must do all your life and with every single thing you hear and read. What are the true things, and what are not? What is good, and what is rubbish? Everything you encounter in life, everything you read, you have to use your own noggin, my girl."

"Well," I tell her, "it doesn't matter, since I don't know how to read."

"You'll learn," she says. "And since you're going to America, you'll also need to learn to read English." She says this matter-of-factly, as if she is telling me I'll need to gather eggs from the nest if we're to have breakfast.

"I can't learn all that!" I protest. "It's too hard. I haven't the wits for it."

She puts one hand on her hip and gives me a good looking-at. "Child," she says, with a shake of her head, "if there's one thing you don't lack, it's wits. You'll learn to read, and you'll start right now, because there's a lot of catching up to do." She escorts me out of the bedchamber and then shoves me toward Bjørn, who is standing there with a book under his arm.

"If you like, Margit, I will help you . . ." He trails off when he sees my scowl, then takes a step back. "I remember how we met!" he says suddenly. "You're the girl—that's the same scowl—" And he starts laughing, which, of course, makes me scowl even harder.

Then I hear Greta's voice saying, "Why don't you show the goodness in you? You're as full of it as a hive is of honey." Do I have goodness inside me? For the first time in ever so long, I think that I might.

East of the Sun, West of the Moon

I n the story of the girl and her prince, after the girl had gained entry into the castle, and the prince had finally overcome the sleeping potion that had been given him, and after the troll hag had tried and failed to wash the tallow out of his shirt and had flown into such a rage that she burst, the prince and the girl (now his bride) took as much gold and silver as they could carry and moved far away from the castle that lay east of the sun and west of the moon. And that was the end of their story.

My story has not come to an end at all, but a sort of beginning. This is my story now, to make of it what I will.

Here I sit with Bjørn, learning to read, and that's a beginning of sorts. He has a book we're studying from, and I've brought along Papa's book. Someday, when I learn enough, I want to read it myself. Meanwhile, it sits on my lap, unopened.

It's hard to concentrate on the page when everyone says that we might get our first glimpse of America any moment— if the fog would lift, that is. Anyway, this reading business is going slowly. Just like the parson's wife, Bjørn says he thinks

I need spectacles, because of how close I hold the book to my eyes.

But we are working at it when here comes the captain, shouting, "Get the speaking-trumpet! Light the turpentine torch!"

Bjørn and I lift our heads to see that the fog has become so thick that you can't see from here to the other end of the *Columbus*. We've also become aware, as have the other passengers, all tense and silent, of a deep rumbling sound.

"What is it?" someone asks.

"A steamer," the captain answers darkly. "Where's that fiddler?" he shouts. "Roust him out!"

The mate shouts into the speaking-trumpet, the torch is lit, and soon the fiddle starts to sing, slicing the fog like a sheep shears through wool.

There's the ringing of a bell, a signal from the steamer. But the rumble comes nearer. Still, we see nothing—the fog takes care of that.

The fiddle's music calls plaintively out over the water. "We are here," it seems to sing, over and over. "Here we are."

Now the rumble is beside us.

There's a collective gasp that turns to a sigh as the fog seems to take the form of a ship, then passes by. It takes but a heartbeat for the ship to pass us, and everyone breathes again.

After a time the sun breaks through the fog bank, as if the music cut a hole for it. Bjørn and I set aside the book to watch how the sun dots the ocean with bright patches of light, making brilliant stepping stones leading all the way to America, maybe.

Excited shouting makes us follow the crowd's pointing fingers off toward the horizon.

"Do you see it?" Bjørn says. He turns to me. "Can you see? It's land!" He jumps up to join the others at the rail. "America!" he cries.

It's too far away for me to see—perhaps the parson's wife is right about spectacles—but I don't need to see it. I can picture it, like the castle that lies east of the sun and west of the moon, all aglitter with possibility.

I listen to the *Columbus* plowing its way through the water, and let the wind pour over me and past me. The ship moves steadily west, and I feel myself moving steadily forward, toward something, although I don't know what it will be.

I don't suppose it will all be golden stepping stones. There is, after all, Death to dodge. I can't imagine it will be easy to avoid speaking the Lord's Prayer while living in a parson's home, but I've done other hard things in my life. And then there's the Black Book I'm bringing—into a parsonage! Well, I can't say how that will be.

I have many more questions than answers, which Mor has

said is the way of life. Will I find Papa? Or will Death catch up to me first? Will I ever see Spinning Girl, my own dear sister, again? This key around my neck—what is it for? What will Papa's book say? And will I, *can* I, ever be a good person?

I am wondering all this when who should come and stand over me but Grace.

"You're not over there"—she gestures behind her at the crowd gathered at the rail—"looking at America."

"I can't see it." I point to my eyes. "I've been told my eyes are bad."

"I don't want to see it," she says. "I never wanted to go there." She pulls the hairbrush from her pocket and shakes it at me. "By the way, I've never gotten a single coin from this worthless thing."

"I'm sorry," I tell her. And I mean it.

She sits down next to me. "You know," she says, laughing, "this silly hairbrush is the only thing that kept me from tearing my hair out by the fistful. I was so angry with Papa for taking us away from home. I didn't want to go. Oh, I really did not. I was angry with him. Angry at everyone! The only thing that kept me from throwing myself into the sea was trying to get gold to fall from my hair!"

This makes me laugh. "It's very pretty," I tell her, and then surprise myself by saying, "Let me braid it for you."

So we sit in the fading light, and I take her hair in my hand

and begin to braid, in the way I remember Spinning Girl braiding mine.

"You must be happy to be almost to America," she says to me.

"Yes, I suppose I should be," I answer.

After I have made one long braid, I wind it around on top of Grace's head like a crown, pinning it with her hairpins. "Why didn't you want to go to America?" I ask her.

"Why, because of my friends! I had to leave them all behind!"

"Maybe you can make new ones," I tell her, "though I am hardly qualified to give advice on the matter."

"Perhaps you and I could be friends," she says.

I can only nod, for suddenly my eyes are full of tears. A symptom of my bad eyes, must be. I wipe them dry and look out at the sea.

At that moment, sea and sky go dark and seem to disappear altogether. Then, as if by magic, they are rekindled, this time with a pale gleam—not like daylight, yet not dark night either. It's the moon, rising up full behind us, casting a blue glow over all the world as we sail toward the last of the sun.

Though I don't know everything about my past, nor do I know what the future will bring, right now I know I'm just where I belong: sailing on a perfect ocean of light, east of the sun and west of the moon.

Margi Preus's great-great-grandparents
Linka and Herman Preus, c. 1850.

Author's Note

I went back downstairs again, bringing with me a pretty farmer girl, Margit, whom Herman and I had thought about taking as our maid ... I said that I knew she was alone and that she did not have anyone to support her, and if I could do her a favor by engaging her, then I would do it.

—from *Linka's Diary*

The idea for this story came from those few lines in my great-great-grandmother's diary. Linka Preus was a young wife when she and her husband, Herman, a Lutheran pastor, sailed from Norway to America on the *Columbus* in 1851. But who was this pretty farmer girl? And why was she traveling alone with no prospects in America? These were questions that intrigued me but for which I could find no historical answers. So I invented her story.

Although Astri's story is fictional, the circumstances of the story are based on historical reality.

"America fever" was spreading in Norway, largely because of the lack of opportunities for an increasing population. Supporting large families on farms with poor, rocky soil and a short growing season was challenging. Sometimes girls, by age fifteen considered adults, went or were sent away to other farms to work as dairymaids.

Vaccines for smallpox and other deadly scourges had been introduced (which contributed to the increase in population), but many illnesses remained poorly understood or not understood at all. Among them are some that play roles in this story.

RICKETS

I n nineteenth-century Norway, the childhood illness of rickets was common but misunderstood. Babies born healthy would gradually sicken, developing enlarged heads, black teeth, and jelly-soft bones. Unable to crawl or walk or sometimes even roll over, they wailed in misery. If left untreated, the bowed legs, curved backs, and skeletal deformities endured by rickets sufferers could persist into adulthood.

Since there was no explanation or cure for the ailment, it was not unusual for distraught parents to turn to magical means for help. Various ritual remedies were often tried, and sometimes the *huldrefolk* were blamed. An old persistent belief was that the hidden people (or trolls) stole healthy babies and replaced them with their own monstrous children. These exchanged babies were known as changelings, and various methods meant to entice the trolls to return the stolen baby might be taken, includ-

ing thrashings, burning, and threatening to leave the changeling on the trash heap. It was hoped the trolls would be so
offended by this mistreatment that they would come to rescue
their own child and return the human baby at the same time.

Now we understand that vitamin D is essential for normal
childhood development and must be supplemented in children living in countries where so many months are spent
without sunshine. In this story, Astri was probably saved by
the doses of sunlight she was given, while her twin grew more
and more sickly at home in the dark cottage.

TETANUS [LOCKJAW]

Tetanus is also known as lockjaw because the symptoms
often begin with spasms of the jaw. Infection usually occurs
with contamination of a wound by a bacterium that produces a
neurotoxin that causes painful tightening of the muscles all over
the body. The spasms can be so powerful that they tear muscles
or cause fractures of the spine. Untreated, an infected person
can die from breathing problems due to muscle spasms or from
other complications. Svaalberd's case progresses perhaps more
rapidly than probable, but his symptoms are real, and before
the disease was understood and vaccine and treatment were
available, death from tetanus was likely.

CHOLERA

Cholera, also poorly understood, was a scourge on immigrant ships. The disease spread easily in unsanitary and crowded conditions. Those who died, sometimes in just hours from the onset of the disease, generally succumbed to severe dehydration. It was known as the Blue Death because the skin and lips of a patient turned a grayish blue due to the loss of fluids. Although there was no cholera aboard the *Columbus,* many immigrant ship passengers at the time suffered from it.

ABOUT THE BLACK BOOK

In an era when so many illnesses and diseases were not understood, and when the closest doctor might be sixty or more miles distant, people turned to what help they could in a crisis.

Folk healers, *kloke koner* or *menn* (wise women or men), were relied upon to help with illnesses, injuries, births, and childhood maladies. These healers had knowledge of herbs and cures, as well as experience with all kinds of ailments, and often gave useful aid. Sometimes, however, it seemed that something *extra* was needed. So there were occasions, especially in the case of undiagnosed childhood illnesses (including rickets), when the *kloke kone* would come to the patient's house and perform rituals, perhaps involving melted lead—preferably taken from church windowsills or church bells at midnight. She might have in her possession a Black Book, containing incantations, charms, and remedies for all sorts of ailments and problems.

These Black Books were in use throughout Norway from the 1500s through the late 1800s. A few of the books made it to America, even though they were considered dangerous, especially to the improperly initiated.

Although belief in supernatural beings and magical cures was declining during this time, "an almost unbelievable number of precautions, remedies, and occult tricks" were still in use among less-educated farm folk, according to P. C. Asbjørnsen, a nineteenth-century folklorist. Also deeply religious, these simple farm folk "found no conflict between folk beliefs and the pious Christian faith that they observed with equal devotion," Kathleen Stokker points out in *Remedies and Rituals*.

ABOUT THE CHARMS, SPELLS, AND CURSES

The spells, chants, incantations, and curses used in this book are found in the following sources: *The Black Books of Elverum*, edited and translated by Mary Rustad; *Remedies and Rituals: Folk Medicine in Norway and the New Land*, by Kathleen Stokker; and *Scandinavian Folk Belief and Legend*, edited by Reimund Kvideland and Henning K. Sehmsdorf. (Full references are in bibliography.) The descriptions that the goatman and

Astri give of the Black Book's contents are adapted from an 1816 history as translated by Kathleen Stokker. According to the quote, the Black Book was the "horrifying, nefarious tome known by everyone in the countryside as Cyprianus, whereby one can conjure up and put down the devil and get him to do just as one commands, and whose pages teach how to recover lost goods, cure all kinds of disease, remove curses, find buried treasure, turn back the attacks of snakes and dogs, and more."

ABOUT THE FOLKTALES

This story relies heavily on the Norwegian folk and fairy tales my father used to tell in Norwegian (translating into English for us kids as he went along). As is common with such stories, some of these are known in other countries by other names.

Folktales referenced herein, among snippets of others (in no particular order):

— "East of the Sun and West of the Moon"

— "White Bear King Valemon"

— "Soria Moria Castle"

— "The Golden Castle That Hung in the Air"

— "The Three Princesses in the Mountain-in-Blue"

— "The Companion"

— "The Hare Who Was Married"

- —"The Boy with the Beer Keg"
- —"The Twelve Wild Ducks"
- —"Peik"
- —"The Three Billy Goats Gruff Who Went Up into the Hills to Get Fat"
- —"Dapplegrim"
- —"Twigmuntus, Cowbelliantus, Perchnosius" (Swedish)

FROM THE DIARY

Some portions of the story that take place on board the *Columbus* are directly lifted from my great-great-grandmother Linka's diary, including the sandwich-snatching rooster, the description of the Sunday shipboard congregants, and the passage about being "happy with the happy." Linka also describes a Halling dance, storms, seasickness, and a steamer that passes by in heavy fog.

The sentiments about immigrating to America expressed by the pastor in the chapter "We Come to a Church" may have been picked up from a pastoral letter dated 1837 by Bishop Jacob Neumman titled "A Word of Admonition to the Peasants in the Diocese of Bergen Who Desire to Emigrate," according to the book *The Promise of America*, by Odd Lovoll. Another widely spread rumor was that Norwegians were taken to Turkey and sold as slaves.

❧ FROM LINKA'S DIARY ❧

❧❧❧❧

TOP:
Sketch of a Norwegian
village in a valley.

BOTTOM:
Sketch of an old woman.

OPPOSITE:
A page from the diary.

❧❧❧❧

Den 19d October.

God Gud- hvor deiligt Du lader os have
det om Dagen-ja- om Natten ogsaa.
allerede er vi langt ud Høstens Tid, og her
er saa varmt, som den hineste Sommer-
morgen- ret en herlig Tid er denne saakaldte
'Indensommer' eller Eftersommer. I Au-
gust og September havde vi ilt ofte dueligt
koldt mangen Morgen var Marken hvid
og rimet og Vandpølen ved Brønden var fros-
sen lisskorpe over, med blaae Kind gik
Pigen og stæved ud i Kjøkkeriet om Morg-
nen før hun fik Ovnen til at hed lidt, trak
saa sin Kuffte af bag et en gammel Træ-
skoe hvori puttedes nogle Gløder, saa et
Par tørre Vedstykker for hermed at faae
Ovnen ind hos os til at dirre, saa vi ikke
skulle fryse naar vi ville lette paa vore
Dovne Personer, men nu fryser hverken
hun eller vi, nu er det saa varmt at Vinduer-
ne staae aabne om Dagen, og hvad der er saa
velsignet deiligt er, at den foregaaende
Kuld har taget Mygger, Vægglusen og
alle disse venneelige Kryb og Dyr bort,
saa vi rigtig nu kan Kose os i denne be-
hagelige Aarstid. Hermann er paa sin
lange Nordreise - vi vil takke Gud fordi
Han lader Dig have det saa godt og mildt-
De 2d foregaaende Høste, vi have været her
har vi kun hørt tale om Denne Indensommer

GLOSSARY AND APPROXIMATE PRONUNCIATIONS

ASTRI (AH-stree): girl's name

BJØRN (BYORN): boy's name; also means "bear"

DALE-GUDBRAND (DOLL-eh good-BRAHND): an eleventh-century pagan chieftain of central Norway who was converted to Christianity by King Olaf

FJORD (fyord): a waterway, often narrow, that leads to the sea

GOD DAG (GOO DAG): good day

GRETA (GREH-ta): girl's name

HALLINGDAL (HALL-ing-dahl): a specific valley in Norway

HUTETU (HOO-tee-too): troll's nonsense word

I JESU NAVN (ee YAY-zu NAVN): in Jesus's name

JA (ya): yes

KLOKE KONE (KLOH-keh KOH-neh): wisewoman; healer

KNÄKKEBRØD (KNEK-eh-breh): cracker-like bread

KRONER (KRO-ner): monetary unit

MOR KLOSTER (moor KLOS-ter): Mother Kloster

MUS (MOOSE): mouse

ODIN (o-dinn): a major god in Norse mythology; father of gods and men

SETER (SAY-ter): mountain cheese farm

SKILLING (SHIL-ling): small coin

SVAALBERD (SVAAHL-baird): a name

SVEKK (SVEK): weakness

TAKK FOR SIST (tuck for sisst): thanks for the last time

TELEMARK (TEL-eh-mark): an area (now a county) in Norway

Select Bibliography

BOOKS

Altar Book of the Norwegian Evangelical Lutheran Church: A translation. Minneapolis, MN: Augsburg Publishing House. 1915.

Asbjørnsen, P. Chr., og Jørgen Moe. *Folke Og Huldre Eventyr*. Bind I og II. Oslo, Norway: Gyldendal Norsk Forlag. 1932 (first published in 1845).

Asbjørnsen, Peter Christen, and Jørgen Moe. *East o' the Sun and West o' the Moon: 59 Norwegian Folk Tales from the Collection of Peter Christen Asbjørnsen and Jørgen Moe*. Translated by George Webbe Dasent. New York: Dover Publications. 1970 (translation of Asbjørnsen and Moe's *Popular Tales from the Norse*, as published by David Douglas in 1888).

Asbjørnsen, Peter Christen, and Jørgen Moe. *Norwegian Folktales*. Translated by Pat Shaw and Carl Norman. New York: Pantheon Books. 1982.

Bergland, Betty, and Lori Ann Lahlum, editors. *Norwegian American Women: Migration, Communities, and Identities* St. Paul, MN: Minnesota Historical Society Press. 2011.

Booss, Claire, editor. *Scandinavian Folk and Fairy Tales*. New York: Avenal Books. 1984.

Briggs, Katharine. *The Vanishing People: Fairy Lore and Legends*. New York: Pantheon Books. 1978.

Gesme, Ann Urness. *Between Rocks and Hard Places: Traditions, Customs, and Conditions in Norway During the 1800s, Emigration from Norway, the Immigrant Community in America*. Hastings, MN: Caragana Press. 1993.

Hamsun, Knut. *Growth of the Soil*. Translated by W. W. Worster. New York: Alfred A. Knopf. 1921.

Koren, Elisabeth. *The Diary of Elisabeth Koren, 1853–1855*. Translated and edited by David T. Nelson. Northfield, MN: Norwegian-American Historical Association. 1955.

Kvideland, Reimund, and Henning K. Sehmsdorf, editors. *Scandinavian Folk Belief and Legend*. Minneapolis, MN: University of Minnesota Press. 1988.

Lees, J. A., and W. J. Clutterbuck. *Three in Norway by Two of Them*. Oslo, Norway: Aschehoug. 1995 (first published in 1882).

Lovoll, Odd. *The Promise of America: A History of the Norwegian-American People*. Minneapolis, MN: University of Minnesota Press. 1984.

The Lutheran Hymnal. Evangelical Lutheran Synodical Conference of North America. St. Louis, MO: Concordia Publishing House. 1941.

Milford, John. *Norway and Her Laplanders in 1841*. London: John Murray. 1842.

Preus, Linka. *Linka's Diary: A Norwegian Immigrant Story in Word and Sketches*. Edited by Marvin G. Slind and Gracia Grindal. Minneapolis, MN: Lutheran University Press. 2008.

Preus, Linka. *Linka's Diary on Land and Sea, 1845–1864*. Translated and edited by Johan Carl Keyser Preus and Diderikke Margrethe Preus. Minneapolis, MN: Augsburg Publishing House. 1952.

Rustad, Mary, editor and translator. *The Black Books of Elverum*. Lakeville, MN: Galde Press. 2010.

Simpson, Jackson, editor and translator. *Scandinavian Folktales*. London: Penguin. 1988.

Stokker, Kathleen. *Remedies and Rituals: Folk Medicine in Norway and the New Land*. St. Paul, MN: Minnesota Historical Society Press. 2007.

INTERVIEWS

Lovoll, Odd. Personal interview. St. Olaf College, Northfield, MN: November 29, 2012.

Acknowledgments

I owe both gratitude and apology to P. C. Asbjørnsen and Jørgen Moe, whose collected Norwegian folk stories I freely pillaged. The same goes to my great-great-grandmother Linka Preus, from whose diary I borrowed without her permission or approval.

Thank you to all those who helped with information and expertise, including Kathleen Stokker for her wonderful books about Norway, especially *Remedies and Rituals: Folk Medicine in Norway and the New Land*. A shout-out to immigration expert Odd Lovoll, a hearty handshake to Dr. Scott Wolff, and *tusen takk* to infectious disease and Norwegian ephemera expert Dr. Johan Bakken.

Thanks to Rachel Vagts at the Luther College Library for help with and permission to use images from Linka's sketchbooks. Thanks also to Lutheran University Press for permission to use snippets of *Linka's Diary*. And thanks to the fabulous Vesterheim Norwegian-American Museum just for existing.

To all those who read and commented on the story as it progressed, including my writing group, especially Ann Treacy, thank you. May you each possess a pair of scissors that snips and plays in the air, and everywhere it goes, it edits. To readers Jean Walsh, Kathy Bogen, Catherine Preus, enthusiastic husband Arno, and especially to astute young readers Emma Kathleen Connell and Laurel McBeath Clark, I wish you bookshelves that never run out of books. To my magic-working agent, Stephen Fraser, may you possess a mailbox to which you only have to say, "Mailbox, stuff thyself," and it will be full of fabulous manuscripts.

I am over the moon to have the privilege of working with the wonderful folks at Abrams/Amulet. Thanks to Sara Corbett and Chad Beckerman for spinning magic with book design, and to Lilli Carré for working more magic with cover art. For weaving it all together, thanks to Jason Wells, Laura Mihalick, Jen Graham, and especially to Howard Reeves, whose like cannot be found east of the sun or west of the moon.

MARGI PREUS

is the author of the Newbery Honor winner
Heart of a Samurai and *Shadow on the Mountain*, which
School Library Journal gave a starred review and called a
"gripping tale that keeps readers riveted to the end." She has
traveled the globe to research her novels and, along the
way, has made friends in Japan, Norway, and many
other places. She lives in Duluth, Minnesota.
Visit her online at margipreus.com.

This book was designed by Sara Corbett and art directed by Chad W. Beckerman. The text in this book is set in Farnham, a serif type family created by Christian Schwartz in 2004. Schwartz based his design on the work of the eccentric eighteenth-century German type designer Johann Fleischman. Farnham is characterized by bold, wedge-shaped serifs on characters such as the lowercase "b" and "u," ball terminals on the lowercase "f" and "y," and playful treatment of italics, especially the uppercase "Q." These ideas were revolutionary in Fleischman's time, and contribute to Farnham's characteristic "sparkle."

The type used on the cover and for the dropcaps at the begining of each chapter is hand-drawn. The chapter titles are set in Gothic Blond.

The cover illustration was created by Lilli Carré.

This book was printed and bound by RR Donnelley in Crawfordsville, Indiana. Its production was overseen by Kathy Lovisolo.